MICHAEL KANE

By nightfall we made out the Gates by means of Deimos's very dim moonlight. They were mainly natural cave mouths widened and made taller by crude workmanship. They were dark and gloomy, and I could understand Darnad's warning.

Only my mission—to rescue the woman I loved but would never be able to make mine—would induce me to enter.

We left our faithful mount outside to fend for himself until we returned—if ever we should.

Then we entered the Caves of Darkness.

MICHAEL MOORCOCK

WARRIORS OF MARS

Originally published under the pen-name of Edward P. Bradbury

ACE BOOKS, NEW YORK

Originally published in 1965 as *Warriors of Mars*
under the pen-name of "Edward P. Bradbury." Sub-
sequent editions published under the title *City of the
Beast* and acknowledged as the work of Michael
Moorcock.

WARRIORS OF MARS

An Ace Book / published by arrangement with
the author

PRINTING HISTORY
Daw Books edition published 1979
Ace edition/March 1991

ISBN: 0-441-87339-1

Ace Books are published by The Berkley Publishing Group,
200 Madison Avenue, New York, New York 10016.
The name "ACE" and the "A" logo
are trademarks belonging to Charter Communications, Inc.

PRINTED IN THE UNITED STATES OF AMERICA

10 9 8 7 6 5 4 3 2 1

*Dedicated to the memories of
Edgar Rice Burroughs and
H. G. Wells, with thanks
and with admiration*

TABLE OF CONTENTS

INTRODUCTION TO THE ORIGINAL EDITION

I was spending the season at Nice—being fortunate enough to possess a small private income. It was the lovely summer of 1964 and the crowds were greater than normal—so much so that I found it necessary to take long walks along the coast and inland if I desired a little comparative solitude.

I am thankful now to those crowds—had they not forced me away from the main centers I should never have met Michael Kane, that strange, enigmatic character in whose life I was soon to become closely involved.

Lemontagne is situated about twelve miles along the coast from Nice. A small but picturesque village on the cliff-top, I had discovered it several years before and found it a pleasant, restful place. There was a white-walled café where the coffee was excellent and from its terrace you could look out over the blue Mediterranean. Unspoiled by tourists, untouched by the passing of time, Lemontagne with its café-terrace was a peaceful haven for me.

The date, I remember, was July 15th—one of the best days of the year, warm and bright and soporific.

I was sitting at my usual table sipping a cool Pernod and looking out over the blue, blue sea when I first noticed the big man. He came and sat down at a table close to mine, ordering a light beer in a quiet, American accent.

A tall, slim-hipped giant, bronzed and handsome and with the appearance of a man of action, he looked like a young god in those surroundings. Yet there was a haunted look about the eyes that seemed to speak of some strange tragedy—perhaps mystery—in his past.

I am something of a literary dabbler, having already written one or two small volumes of travel and reminiscence, and my literary instincts were instantly alerted. My curiosity overcame normal good manners and I decided to try to engage him in conversation.

"A pleasant day, sir," I said.

"Very pleasant." His tone was friendly but distant, his smile somewhat half-hearted.

"You are an American, I would guess. Are you staying in the village?"

He nodded abstractedly, then looked away and stared out to sea. Perhaps it was boorish of me to continue—perhaps I intruded. But if I had not I should have deprived myself of an incredible experience and missed the strangest story that has ever been told to me.

When the waiter came for my next order I told him to bring the American another beer. When it came I took my own drink over to his table and asked if I might join him.

"Forgive me," he said, looking up suddenly and giving me one of those friendly, half-sad, mysterious smiles which were soon to become familiar. "I was dreaming. By all means sit down. I would like someone to talk to."

"Have you been here long?" I asked.

"Where—on Earth?"

It was a strangely startling answer. I laughed. "No, no—of course not. In the village."

"No," he said, "not long. Though"—he sighed deeply—"far too long, I regret to say. You are English, aren't you?"

"Actually born in New England," I said, "but English by adoption. Where are you from in America?"

"America? Oh, Ohio originally."

I was baffled by his oddly oblique replies and his detached way of speaking. Why had he wondered if I meant the planet itself when I asked him if he had been in the village very long? The question piqued my curiosity further.

"Do you work in America?" I pressed on.

"I did once, yes." Suddenly he looked directly at me, his diamond-blue eyes seeming to bore into my brain. I felt as if an electric current had surged through me. Then he continued: "That was the whole start of it, I suppose. I could tell you a tale that would send you running to phone the nearest lunatic asylum and have me put away!"

"You intrigue me. By the look of you it is some tragedy. Have you been crossed in love—is that it?" I was beginning to wonder just how impertinent my rising curiosity was making me. But he did not seem offended.

"In a sense, you could say that. My name is Michael Kane. Does that mean anything to you?"

"It rings a faint bell," I admitted.

"Professor Michael Kane of the Chicago Special

Research Institute." He sighed again, his manner retrospective. "We were doing top secret research on matter transmitters."

"Matter transmitters?"

"I shouldn't really be telling you this, but it doesn't seem important now. We were trying to build a machine that, by a combination of electronics and nucleonics, could break down the atoms of an object and translate them into a series of waves that could be transmitted across great distances like radio-waves. There was a receiver which could, theoretically, retranslate the waves back into the object."

"You mean an apple could be broken down into particles, transmitted like, say, a radio-picture, and become the same apple again at the receiving end? I have read something about it, now you mention it. I had thought such a machine was still only theoretical."

"It was until comparatively recently—in your recent past, that is."

"My past? Isn't it essentially the same as yours?" I was again surprised.

"I am coming to that," he said. "If perfected, a machine of the type we've discussed could take even a *human being,* break him down into atoms, transmit him across any selected distance, and have the 'receiver' at the other end put him together again!"

"Astounding! How did you make this discovery?"

"It became possible to build such a machine following completion of some research on lasers and masers. I will not bore you with a series of obscure equations, but our work on light-waves and radio-waves was of great help. I was the physicist in charge of the work. I was obsessed with the idea . . ." His voice trailed off and he looked thoughtfully down at the table, clenching his long-fingered hands together tightly.

"What happened?" I asked eagerly.

"We got the machine working. We sent a few rats and mice through it—successfully. Then we had to test it on a human subject. It was dangerous—we couldn't ask for volunteers."

"So you decided to test it yourself?"

He smiled. "That's right. I was so eager to prove it would really work, you see, though I was convinced it would." He paused, then added: "But it *didn't* work."

"You survived, however," I pointed out. "Unless I'm talking to a ghost!"

"You're closer to the truth than you think, my friend. Where would you say I went after I entered the matter transmitter?"

"Well, it seems natural that you went to the receiver and were—um—put together again."

"You think me sane?" Again this strange man was off at a slight tangent.

"Eminently sane," I said.

"You would not say I had the appearance or manner of a liar?"

"Far from it. Where is this leading? Where did you go?"

"Believe me," he said seriously. *"I left this planet altogether!"*

I gasped. For a moment I thought my confidence in his sanity and his word had been misplaced. But then I saw that it had not been. His whole manner was that of a man speaking sane truth. "You went into *space?*" I said.

"I went *through* space—and time as well, I think. *I went to Mars, my friend.*"

"Mars!" I was now even more incredulous. "But how could you have survived? Mars is lifeless—a waste of dust and lichen!"

"Not this Mars, my friend."

"There is *another* Mars?" I raised my eyebrows.

"In a sense, yes. The planet I visited was not, I am convinced, the Mars we can see through our telescopes. It was an older Mars, eons in the past, yet still ancient. It is my theory that our own ancestors originated on the planet and came here when Mars was dying millions of years ago!"

"You mean you met people on the Red Planet?"

"People very similar to us. More—I encountered a strange romantic civilization totally unlike any we have ever had on Earth. Perhaps our most ancient legends hint at it—legends that we brought with us from Mars when our race fled from there to Earth and degenerated into savagery before beginning the upward climb towards civilization again. Ah, it was beautiful, fantastic, breath-taking—a place where a man could *be* a man and survive and be recognized for his true qualities of character and prowess. And then there was Shizala . . ."

I recognized the look in his eyes this time. "So there was a woman," I said softly.

"Yes, there was a woman. A girl—young, ravishingly attractive, a tall Martian girl, an aristocrat from a line that would have made the dynasties of Egypt appear trifling by comparison. She was Princess of Varnal, City of the Green Mists, with its spires and colonnades, its ziggurats and domes, its strong, slen-

der people—and the finest fighting men in that martial
world . . ."

"Go on," I breathed, entranced.

"It seems like a splendid dream now." He smiled
sadly. "A dream that I may yet recapture." Then his
lips set firmly and his diamond-blue eyes gleamed
with determination. "I must!"

"And *I* must hear the whole story," I said excitedly. Although my reason rejected his fantastic tale,
my emotions accepted it. He was right, I was almost
sure. "Will you come with me to my hotel? I have a
tape-recorder there. I should like to hear everything
you can tell me—and record it."

"You are certain I'm not mad or lying?"

"Fairly certain," I said with a self-deprecating
smile. "I am not quite sure. You must let me judge
when I have heard all."

"Very well." He got up abruptly.

I am by no measure a short man, but he was a full
head and shoulders taller.

"I should like you to believe me," he said.
"And . . ." He broke off, controlling himself from saying something he evidently dearly wanted to say.

"What is it?" I urged as we settled the bill and
began to walk to the nearby taxi rank, where stood
one decrepit cab.

"I cannot return to my laboratory, you understand," he said. "And yet to build another transmitter
would be expensive. I—I need help."

"I am a man of comfortable means," I told him,
leaning forward in the cab to give the driver instructions. "I may be able to help in some way."

"You will probably not believe me," he said with

that half-smile of his, "but it will be a relief to find an ear which is at least sympathetic."

We were driven back to my hotel in Nice—the Hotel de la Mer. In my suite I ordered a meal to be brought to us. As ever, the food was excellent and had a mellowing effect on us both. When we had finished, I switched on my machine and he began to talk.

As I have said, I could not at first unreservedly believe his strange narrative. Yet, as he spoke on, the tape recording all he said, I became convinced that he was neither a madman nor a liar. He had experienced everything he told me. When he finished speaking, after many hours long into the night, I felt that I, too, had experienced the wild and remarkable adventures of Michael Kane, American physicist and— *Warrior of Mars!*

What you are about to read is essentially what he told me. The few omissions and clarifications I have made are in the cause of readability and to conform to the laws of Britain and the United States—laws for the most part involving scientific secrets. You must judge Kane as I judged him. However you feel, I must add, do not condemn him at once as a liar, for if you had seen him as I saw him in that hotel room in Nice, speaking in flowing, controlled sentences, his eyes staring up at the ceiling as if at Mars herself, and his whole attitude one of reminiscence, changing with the moods he felt as he recalled this scene or that, you would have believed him as implicitly as I did.

E. P. B.
Chester Square
London, S.W.1.

April 1965

CHAPTER ONE

MY DEBT TO M. CLARCHET

THE Matter Transmitter is both villain and hero of this story (began Kane), for it took me to a world where I felt more at home than I shall ever feel here. It brought me to a wonderful girl whom I loved and who loved me—and then took it all away again.

But I had better begin nearer the beginning.

I was born, as I told you, in Ohio—in Wynnsville—a small, pleasant town that never changed much. Its only unusual feature was in the person of M. Clarchet, a Frenchman who had settled there shortly after the First World War. He lived in a large place on the outskirts of town. M. Clarchet was a cosmopolitan, a Frenchman of the old school—short, very straight-backed, with a typically French, waxed moustache and a rather military way of walking.

To be honest, M. Clarchet was something of a caricature to us and seemed to illustrate everything we had learned about the French in our dime novels and comic books. Yet I owe my life to M. Clarchet, though I wasn't to realize it until many years after the old gentleman had passed on, and when I found myself suddenly transported to Mars . . . But again I am getting ahead of myself.

Clarchet was an enigma even to me though, as boy and youth, I probably knew him better than anyone else. He had been, he said, a fencing master at the Court of the Tsar of Russia before the Revolution and had had to leave in a hurry when the Bolsheviks took over.

He had settled in Wynnsville directly because of this experience. It had seemed to him at the time that the whole world was in chaos and was being turned upside down. He had found a small town that was never likely to change much—and he liked it. The way of life he led now was radically different from the one he had been used to, and it seemed to suit him.

We first met when I had accepted a dare by my young pals to climb the fence of his house and see if I could observe what M. Clarchet was up to. At that time we were all convinced he was a spy of some description! He had caught me, but instead of shooting me, as I half-expected, he had laughed good-naturedly and sent me on my way. I liked him at once.

Soon after that we kids had a phase which was a sequel to seeing Ronald Colman in *The Prisoner of Zenda*. We all became Ruperts and Rudolfs for a time. With long canes for swords, we fenced one another to exhaustion—not very skilfully but with a lot of enthusiasm!

On a sunny afternoon in early summer, it so happened that I and another boy, Johnny Bulmer, were duelling for the throne of Ruritania just outside M. Clarchet's house. Suddenly there came a great shout from the house and we wheeled in astonishment.

"Non! Non! Non!" The Frenchman was plainly ex-

asperated. "That ees wrong, wrong, wrong! That ees not how a gentleman fences!"

He rushed from his garden and seized my cane, adopting a graceful fencing stance and facing a startled Johnny, who just stood there with his mouth open.

"Now," he said to Johnny, "you do ze same, *oui?*"

Johnny inelegantly copied his posture.

"Now, you thrust—so!" The cane darted out in a flicker of movement and stopped just short of Johnny's chest.

Johnny copied him—and was parried with equal swiftness. We were amazed and delighted by this time. Here was a man who would have been a good match for Rupert of Hentzau.

After a while M. Clarchet stopped and shook his head. "It ees no good with thees sticks—we must have real foils, *non?* Come!"

We followed him into the house. It was well furnished though not lavishly. In a special room at the top we found more to make us gasp.

Here was an array of blades such as we'd never even imagined! Now I know them to be foils and *épées* and sabres, plus a collection of fine, antique weapons— claymores, scimitars, Samurai swords, broadswords, Roman short swords—the *gladius*—and many, many more.

M. Clarchet waved a hand at the fascinating display of weapons. "Zere! My collection. Zey are sweet, ze little swords, *non?*" He took down a small rapier and handed it to me, handing a similar sword to Johnny. It felt really good, holding that well-balanced sword in my hand. I flexed my wrist, not quite able to get the balance. M. Clarchet took my hand and showed me the correct way of grasping it.

"How would you like to learn properly?" said M. Clarchet with a wink. "I could teach you much."

Was it possible? We were going to be allowed to wield these swords—taught how to sword-fight like the best. I was amazed and delighted—until a thought struck me, and I frowned.

"Oh—we don't have any money, sir. We couldn't pay you and our moms and pops aren't likely to— they're mean enough as it is."

"I do not wish for payment. The skill you acquire from me will be reward enough! Here—I will show you zee simple parry first . . ."

And so he taught us. Not only did we learn how to fence with the modern conventional weapons— foils, *épées* and sabres—but also with the antique and foreign weapons of all shapes, weights, sizes and balances. He taught us the whole of his marvellous art.

Whenever we could, Johnny and I attended M. Clarchet's special Sword Room. He seemed grateful to us, in his way, for the opportunity to pass on his skill, just as we were to him for giving us the chance to learn. By the time we were around fifteen we were both pretty good, and I think I probably had the edge on Johnny, though I say it myself.

Johnny's parents moved to Chicago about that time so I became M. Clarchet's only pupil. When I wasn't studying physics at high school and later at university, I was to be found at M. Clarchet's, learning all I could. And at last the day came when he cried with joy. I had *beaten* him in a long and complicated duel!

"You are zee best, Mike! Better zan any I have known!"

It was the highest praise I have ever received. At university I went in for fencing, of course, and was picked for the American team in the Olympics. But it was a crucial time in my studies and I had to drop out at the last moment.

That was how I learned to fence, anyway. I thought of it in my more depressed moments as rather a purposeless sport—archaic and only indirectly useful, in that it gave me excellently sharp reactions, strengthened my muscles and so on. It was useful in the Army, too, for the physical discipline essential in Army training was already built in to me.

I was lucky. I did well in my studies and survived my military service, part of which was spent fighting the Communist guerrillas in the jungles of Vietnam. By the time I was thirty, I was known as a bright boy in the world of physics. I joined the Chicago Special Research Institute, and because of my ideas on matter transmission was appointed Director of the department responsible for developing the machine.

I remember we were working late on it, enlarging its capacity so that it could take a man.

The neon lights in the lab ceiling illuminated the shining steel and plastic cabinet, the great 'translator cone' directed down at it, and all the other equipment and instruments that filled the place almost to capacity. There were five of us working—three technicians and Doctor Logan, my chief assistant.

I checked all the instruments while Logan and the men worked on the equipment. Soon all the gauges were reading what they should read, and we were ready.

I turned to Doctor Logan and looked at him. He

said nothing as he looked back at me. Then we shook
hands. That was all.

I climbed into the machine. They had tried to talk
me out of it earlier but had given up by this time.
Logan reached for the phone and contacted the team
handling the 'receiver'. This was situated in a lab on
the other side of the building.

Logan told the team we were ready and checked
with them. They were ready, too.

Logan walked to the main switch. Through the little glass panel in the cabinet I saw him switch it on
gravely.

My body began to tingle pleasantly. That was all
at first. It is difficult to describe the weird sensation
I experienced as soon as the transmitter began to
work. It was literally true that every atom of my body
was being torn apart—and it felt like it. I began to
get light-headed; then came the sensation of frightful
pressures building up inside me, followed by the feeling that I was exploding outwards.

Everything went green and I felt as though I was
spreading gently in all directions. Then came a riot
of colors blossoming around me—reds, yellows, pur-
ples, blues.

There was an increasing sense of weightlessness—
*mass*lessness even. I felt I was streaming through
blackness and my mind began to blank out altogether.
I felt I was hurtling over vast distances, beyond time
and space—covering an incredible area of the universe
in every direction in a few seconds.

Then I knew nothing more!

I came to my senses—if senses they were—under
a lemon-colored sun blazing down on me from out of
a deep blue, near-purple sky. It was a color more in-

tense than any I had ever seen before. Had my experience enabled me to see color with greater sharpness?

But when I looked around I realized that it was more than intensity which had changed. I was lying in a field of gently swaying, sweet-smelling ferns. But they were ferns unlike any I had ever seen!

These ferns were an impossible shade of crimson!

I rubbed my eyes. Had the transmitter—or rather the receiver—gone wrong and put me together slightly mixed up, with my color sense in a muddle?

I got up and looked across the sea of crimson ferns.

I gasped.

My whole sight must somehow have been altered!

Cropping at the ferns, with a line of yellowish hills in the background, was a beast as large as an elephant and of roughly the same proportions as a horse. Yet here the similarity to any beast I knew ended. This creature was a mottled shade of mauve and light green. It had three long, white horns curling from its flat, almost catlike head. It had twin, somewhat reptilian, tails spreading to the ground behind it, and it had one huge eye covering at least half the area of its face. This was a faceted eye that shone and glinted in the sunlight. The beast looked rather curiously at me and lifted its head, then began to move towards me.

With, I suspect, a wild yell, I ran. I felt convinced I was experiencing some sort of nightmare or paranoiac delusion as a result of a fault in the transmitter or receiver.

I heard the beast thundering on behind me, giving out a strange mooing sound, and increased my pace as best I could. I found I could run very easily indeed and seemed to be lighter than normal.

Then to one side of me I heard musical laughter,

at once merry and sympathetic. A lilting voice called
something in what was to me a strange, unearthly language, trilling and melodic. In fact, the sound of the
language was so beautiful that it did not seem to need
words.

"Kahsaaa manherra vosu!"

I slowed my pace and looked towards the source
of the voice.

It was a girl—the most wonderful girl I have ever
seen in my life.

Her hair was long, free and golden. Her face was
oval, her white skin clear and fresh. She was naked,
apart from a wispy cloak which curled round her
shoulders and a broad, leather belt around her waist.
The belt held a short sword and a holster from which
jutted the butt of a pistol of some kind. She was tall
and her figure was exquisite. Somehow her nakedness
was not obvious and I accepted it at once. She, too,
was totally unselfconscious about it. I stopped still,
not caring about the beast behind me so long as I
could have a few seconds' glimpse of her.

Again she threw back her head and laughed that
merry laugh.

Suddenly I felt something wet tickling my neck.
Thinking it must be an insect of some sort, I put up
my hand. But it was too large for an insect. I turned.

That strange mauve and green beast, that monster
with the fly-like, cyclops eye, two tails and three
horns, was gently licking me!

Was it tasting me? I wondered vaguely, still concen-
trating on the girl. Judging by the way she was laughing, I thought not.

Wherever I was—in dream or lost world—I knew
that I had fled in panic from a tame, friendly, domes-

tic animal. I blushed and then joined in the girl's laughter.

After a moment I said: "If it's not a rude question, I wonder, ma'am, if you could tell me where I am."

She wrinkled her perfect brow when she heard me and shook her head slowly. *"Uhoi merrash? Civinnee norshasa?"*

I tried again in French but without any luck. Then in German—again no success. Spanish was equally ineffective at producing communication between us. My Latin and Greek were limited, but I tried those, too. I am something of a linguist, picking up foreign tongues quickly. I tried to remember the little Sioux and Apache I had learned during a brief study of the Red Indians at college. But nothing worked.

She spoke a few more words in her language which seemed to me, when I listened very carefully, to have certain faint similarities to classical Sanskrit.

"We are both, it seems, at a loss," I remarked, standing there with the beast still licking me lovingly.

She stretched out a hand for me to take. My heart pounded and I could hardly make myself move. *"Phoresha,"* she said. She seemed to want me to go somewhere with her, and pointed towards the distant hills.

I shrugged, took her hand and went along with her.

So that was how, hand in hand with its loveliest resident, I came to Varnal, City of the Green Mists— most splendid of the splendid Martian cities.

Oh, how many thousands upon thousands of years ago!

CHAPTER TWO

THE ASTOUNDING TRUTH

VARNAL is more real to me, even in my memories, than ever Chicago or New York can be. It
lies in a gentle valley in the hills, which the Martians
term the Calling Hills. Green and golden, they are
covered with slender trees and, when the wind passes
through them, they sound like sweet, distant, calling
voices as one walks past.

The valley itself is wide and shallow and contains
a fairly large, hot lake. The city is built around the
lake, from which rises a greenish steam, a delicate
green that sends tendrils curling around the spires of
Varnal. Most of Varnal's graceful buildings are tall
and white, though some are built of the unique blue
marble which is mined close by. Others have traceries
of gold in them, making them glitter in the sunlight.
The city is walled by the same blue marble, which also
has golden traceries in it. From its towers fly pen-
nants, gay and multicolored, and its terraces are
crowded with its handsome inhabitants, the plainest
of whom would be a sought-after beau or belle in
Wynnsville, Ohio—or, indeed, Chicago or any other
great city of our world.

When I first came upon the city of Varnal, led by that wonderful girl, I gasped in awed admiration. She seemed to accept my gasp as the compliment it was and she smiled proudly, saying something in her then incomprehensible language.

I decided that I could not be dreaming, for my own imagination was simply not capable of creating such a vision of splendor and loveliness.

But where was I? I did not know then. How had I got there? That I still cannot answer fully.

I puzzled over the second question. Evidently the matter transmitter had had a fault. Instead of sending me to the receiver on the other side of the lab building it had sent me hurtling through space—perhaps through time, too—to another world. It could not be Earth—not, at least, the Earth of my own age. Somehow I could not believe it was any Earth, of the past or the future. Yet it could not be the only other obvious planet in our solar system—Mars—for Mars was a dead, arid planet of red dust and lichen. Yet the size of the Sun and the fact that gravity was less here than on Earth seemed to indicate Mars.

It was in a daze of speculation that I allowed the girl to lead me through the golden gates of the city, through its tree-lined streets, towards a palace of shining white stone. People, men and women dressed—if dressed is the word—similarly to the girl, glanced in polite curiosity at my white lab coat and grey pants which I was still wearing.

We mounted the steps of the palace and entered a great hall, hung with banners of many colors, on which were embroidered strange emblems, mythical beasts and words traced out in a peculiar script which also reminded me of Sanskrit.

Five galleries rose around the hall and in the centre a fountain played. The few simply-dressed people who stood conversing in the hall waved cheerfully to the girl and gave me that same look of polite curiosity I had received in the streets.

We walked through the hall, through another doorway and up a spiral staircase of white marble. Here she paused on the landing and opened a door that at first looked like metal but on closer observation proved to be wood of incredible hardness and polish.

The room in which I found myself was quite small. It was barely furnished, with a few rugs of brightly dyed animal skins scattered about and a series of cupboards around the walls.

The girl went to one of these cupboards, opened it and took out two metal circlets in which were set radiant gems of a kind completely unknown to me. She placed one of these on her head and indicated that I should imitate her with the second. I took the circlet and fitted it over my own head.

Suddenly a voice spoke inside my skull. I was astonished for a second, until I realized that here was some kind of telepathic communicator which we physicists had only speculated about.

"Greetings, stranger," said the voice, and I could see the girl's lips move, framing those lovely, alien syllables. "From where do you come?"

"I come from Chicago, Illinois," I said, more to test the device than to convey information which I guessed would be meaningless to her.

She frowned. "Soft sounds and very pleasant, but I do not know that place. Where in Vashu is that?"

"Vashu? Is this city in a land called Vashu?"

"No—Vashu is the whole planet. This city is called

Varnal, capital of the nation of the Karnala, my people."

"Do you have astronomy?" I asked. "Do you study the stars?"

"We do. Why do you ask?"

"Which planet is this in relation to the sun?"

"It is the fourth from the sun."

"Mars! It *is* Mars!" I cried.

"I do not follow you."

"I am sorry. Somehow I have arrived here from the third planet, which we call Earth. That is where Chicago is!"

"But there are no men on Negalu, the third planet. Only steamy jungles and monstrous beasts!"

"How do you know so much about the planet?"

"Our ethercraft have visited it and brought back pictures."

"You have space-ships—but . . ." I was at a loss. This was too incredible for me to accept all at once. I questioned her more closely and soon learned that the Earth her people knew was not the Earth I had left. It seemed to be an Earth that had existed millions of years ago, during the Age of Reptiles. Somehow both space and time had been crossed. That matter transmitter had more to it than we'd guessed!

Another thing puzzled me. The people did not appear to have a great deal of technology visible in the city—yet they had space-ships.

"How could this be?" I asked her.

"We did not build the ethercraft. They were a gift from the Sheev—as were these mind-crowns. We have a science of our own but it cannot compare to the great wisdom and knowledge of the Sheev."

"Who are the Sheev?"

"They are very great and few of them still live. They are remote and of an older race than any on Vashu. Our philosophers speculate on their origin, but we know little about them."

I let that go for the time being and decided it was about the moment to introduce myself.

"I am called Michael Kane," I said.

"I am Shizala, Bradhinaka of the Kanala, and ruler in the absence of the Bradhi."

I learned that the Bradhi was about the equivalent of our 'king', although the title did not suggest that the man who held it possessed absolute power. Perhaps Guide would be a better one—or Protector? Bradhinaka meant, roughly, Princess—daughter of the King.

"And where is the Bradhi?" I asked.

I saw her face become sad and she glanced at the ground.

"My father disappeared two years ago—on a punitive expedition against the Argzoon. He must have been killed or, if he was captured, killed himself. It is better to die than become a prisoner of the Blue Giants."

I expressed my sympathy and did not feel the time right to ask what the Argzoon or Blue Giants were. She was evidently deeply moved by the memory of the loss of her father, but showed great self-control in refusing to burden someone else with her grief.

I felt immediately like trying to offer her some comfort. But, considering I knew nothing of the moral code and customs of her people, that might perhaps have been disastrous.

She touched her circlet. "We only need to wear these for the time being. The Sheev have given us another machine which should be able to teach you our spoken language."

We conversed a little longer and I learned much of Mars—or Vashu, as I was already beginning to think of it.

There were many nations on Mars, some friendly towards the Kanala, some not. They all spoke recognizable versions of the same root language. This is supposedly true of Earth—that our language was originally a common one; but in our case the changes have been extreme. This was not the case, I learned, on Vashu.

Mars's seas still existed, Shizala told me, though apparently they were not so vast as Earth's. Varnal, capital of the Karnala nation, was one of a number of countries, with rather hazily defined borders, which existed on a large land-mass bigger, but in roughly the same geographical position, than the whole of the American continent.

Travel was effected in two main ways. Most ordinary travel relied on the *dahara,* a riding and carriage beast of great strength and endurance. But many nations had a few aircraft. As far as I could make out, these relied on atomics—which none of the Vashu peoples understood. These had not been gifts of the Sheev, I learned, but must once have belonged to the Sheev. They were incredibly ancient by all accounts and could not be replaced when destroyed. Thus they were only used in emergencies. There were also ships incorporating some sort of atomic engine, and sailing ships of various kinds. These plied the few rivers of Vashu—rivers which were shrinking with almost every year that passed.

For arms, the Vashu warriors relied primarily on

the sword. They had guns—Shizala showed me hers.
It was a long-barreled, finely made weapon with a
comfortable grip. I could not quite see what it fired
or on what principle it worked, but as Shizala tried
to explain haltingly I concluded that it was some sort
of laser gun. What an incredible amount of power, I
thought, was packed into its chambers, for we scien-
tists had always argued that a laser hand-gun was out
of the question, since the power required to produce
the laser ray—tightly focused light which could cut
through steel—relied on a very big generator.
Wonderingly, I handed the gun back to her. These
guns, not gifts of the Sheev but probably looted from
their now lost or completely ruined cities by Shizala's
remote ancestors, were also used infrequently, since
once the charge was finally expended it could not be
replaced.

Their *akashasard*—or ethercraft—apparently
numbered five in all. Three of these belonged to the
Karnala and one each to friendly, neighbouring nations—the Iridala and the Walavala. Although there
were pilots who could operate them, none of the folk
of Vashu had any idea how they worked.

Other benefits which a few chosen nations had received from the mysterious Sheev included a longevity
serum which, once taken, did not need to be taken
again. Everyone was allowed to use it and it gave up
to two thousand years of life! Because of this very few
children were born, so the population of Vashu remained comparatively small. No bad thing, I reflected. I could have listened to Shizala for hours, but
at length she stopped my questions with a smile.

"First we must eat. The evening meal will be served
soon. Come."

I followed Shizala as she led me from the little room and down into the main hall, which was now furnished with several large tables at which sat men and women of Kanala, all handsome and beautiful and chatting gaily.

They all rose politely, though not servilely, as Shizala took her place at the head of one of the tables. She indicated the chair on her left and I sat down. The food looked strange but smelled good. Opposite me, on Shizala's right, sat a dark-haired young man, superbly muscled. He wore a simple gold bangle on his right wrist and he put his arm on the table in such a way as to show it off.

Evidently he was proud of it for he wanted me to see it. I guessed it to be a decoration of some kind and thought no more of it.

Shizala introduced the man as Bradhinak—or Prince Telem Fas Ogdai. The name did not sound like a Karnala name, and it soon transpired that Bradhinak Telem Fas Ogdai was from the city of Mishim Tep, a friendly nation some two thousand miles to the south. He was, so it seemed, a witty talker though, of course, I could not understand what he said. Only a person wearing a circlet could communicate with me.

On my left was a pleasant-faced young man with long, almost white, fair hair. He seemed to be making a special effort to make me feel at home, offering food and drink, asking polite questions through Shizala, who translated for us. This was Darnad, Shizala's younger brother. Apparently the succession to the throne of Varnal was determined by sex and not by age.

Darnad was apparently chief Pukan-Nara of Varnal. A Pukan, I learned, was a warrior, and a Pukan-Nara a warrior leader. The chief Pukan-Nara was elected by popular vote—by civilians and warriors alike. I assumed from this that Darnad's position was therefore no honorary one, and that he had earned it through prowess and intelligence. Though he was personable and charming, the people of Varnal did not judge a man merely on his appearance but on his merit and record.

I was already beginning to pick up a few words of the Vashu tongue by the time the meal was over, and we adjourned into an ante-room to drink a beverage called basu, a sweetish drink I found quite palatable but which, frankly, did not at that time seem as good to me as good, old-fashioned coffee. Later I was to discover that basu grew on one and then I preferred it to coffee. Like coffee, it is a mild stimulant.

In spite of the basu, I began to feel quite sleepy and, always alert to her guests' needs, Shizala sensed this.

"I have had a room prepared for you," she telepathed. "Perhaps you would like to retire now."

I admitted that the day's surprising experiences had taken a lot out of me. A servant was called and Shizala went with us up the stairs to the second floor of the palace. A dim bulb burned in the room, giving adequate light.

Shizala showed me a bell-rope very like old-fashioned bell-ropes on Earth. It was close to the bed and was used to summon a servant. She left her circlet behind when she left. Before she did so she told me that anyone could use the circlet and the servant would know how.

The bed consisted of a wide, hard bench, on which was a thin mattress. A large fur rug was laid over this, and it seemed rather too heavy, since the day had been very warm. To some, perhaps, the bed would have been too austere but, as it happened, it was the kind I preferred.

I fell asleep immediately, having shed my clothes, and I awoke only once in the middle of the Martian night—which is, of course, longer than ours—feeling very cold. I had not realized how much the temperature could change. I pulled the rug about me and was soon asleep again.

CHAPTER THREE

THE INVADERS

A female servant entered in the morning, after
knocking lightly on the door. I was standing at
the window looking out over the beautiful streets and
houses of Varnal. At first I felt embarrassed by my
nakedness. But then I realized that there was no need
since it was abnormal here to wear many clothes, and
then, it seemed, only for decoration.

What did continue to embarrass me, however, was
the look of open admiration she gave me as she
handed me my breakfast tray of fruit and basu.

After she had gone I sat down to eat the fruit—a
large one very similar to grape-fruit but with a slightly
less bitter taste—and drink the basu.

I was just finishing when there was another knock
on the door. I called, "Come in!" in English, thinking
that this would do the trick. It did. In walked Shizala,
smiling.

Seeing her again, it seemed that I had dreamed of
her all night, for she was as beautiful—if not more
so—as I remembered her. Her blonde hair was swept
up from her shoulders and back. She had on a black,
gauzy cloak and at her waist was the wide belt con-

taining holstered gun and short sword. These, I gathered, were ceremonial weapons of office, for I could not imagine such a graceful girl having much familiarity with the artifacts of war. On her feet she wore sandals, laced up the calf almost to the knee. That was all she was wearing—but it was enough.

She picked up the circlet she had worn the day before and put it on.

"I thought you might wish to ride around the city and see everything," I heard her voice say in my head. "Would you like that?"

"Very much," I replied. "If you can spare the time."

"It would please me to do so." She gave me a warm smile.

I could not make up my mind whether she felt as attracted to me as I was to her, or whether she was just being normally polite. It was a puzzle which was already beginning to fill a great deal of my thoughts.

"First," she continued, "it would be better if you spent a couple of hours with the Sheev teaching machine. After that you will be able to converse in our language without recourse to these rather clumsy things."

As she led me down corridors and staircases, I asked her why, if the tongue of Vashu were common, there should be such a thing as a language-teaching machine. She replied that it had been designed for use on other planets but, since the other planets in the solar system only appeared to be inhabited by animals, it had never been used.

She led me below ground. The cellars of the palace seemed to go down many levels, but at last we reached a place lighted by the same sort of dim bulb as the

one in my room. These bulbs were also of Sheev man-
ufacture, Shizala told me, and had once burned much
brighter than they did now. The room was small and
contained a single piece of equipment. It was large and
made of metal I did not recognize—probably an alloy.
It glowed a little, adding to the light in the room. It
seemed to consist of a cabinet with an alcove moulded
to accommodate the form of a seated human being.

I could see no other machinery and I would dearly
have loved to strip the cabinet down to see what was
inside—but curbed my impatience.

"Please sit there," said Shizala, indicating the cabinet. "According to what I have been told, the cabinet
will be activated immediately you do so. You may feel
yourself black out, but do not be disturbed."

I did as she asked and, sure enough, as soon as I
was seated the cabinet began to hum softly. A cap
came down from above and fitted itself over my head,
then I began to feel dizzy and soon became unconscious.

I did not know how much time had passed until
I came to, finding myself still seated in the now no
longer activated cabinet. I looked at Shizala a little
dazedly. My head was aching slightly.

"How do you feel?" she asked.

"Fine," I said, getting up.

But I had not said 'fine' at all, I realized. I had said
vrazha—the Martian word that was its nearest equivalent.

I had spoken Martian!

"It works!" I cried. "What sort of machine is it that
can achieve that so swiftly?"

"I do not know. We are content simply to use the
things of the Sheev. We were warned in the far past

never to tamper with their gifts since it might result
in disaster for us! Their mighty civilization once suf-
fered a disaster, but we have only a few legends which
speak of it and they are bound up in talk of supernatural entities in whom we no longer believe."

Respecting what was evidently a deeply rooted custom never to question the Sheev inventions, I remained silent, though every instinct made me want
to get at the language-teaching machine, probably a
highly sophisticated computer containing an hypnotic
device of some kind.

My headache had gone by the time we reached the
upper levels of the palace and walked through the
great hall out into the city. At the bottom of the wide,
white steps two strange beasts were waiting.

They were about the same size as Shire horses—the
famous English Great Horse which had once borne
knights into battle. But horses they were not. Their
origin seemed to stem from the same basic root as
Man! They were ape-like creatures with wide kanga-
roo tails, their hind legs larger than the forelegs. They
were on all fours now and saddles were on their backs.
Their great heads, placid and intelligent, turned to
look at us as we came down the steps.

I had a few`qualms about mounting mine, since it
did bear certain affinities to my own race, but once
aboard it seemed natural that I should ride it. Its back
was wider than that of a horse and involved stretching
one's legs out in front, and cupping the feet in the stir-
rups attached to another part of the harness up ahead.
The saddle had a solid support allowing the rider to
stretch backwards at ease. It was rather like being
seated in a sports car, and was very comfortable.

In a kind of holster on my right were several lances,

though I had no idea of their purpose. I found that by gentle tugs on the reins, the dahara would respond quickly to any command I made.

With Shizala leading the way, we trotted off through the plaza and down the main street of Varnal.

The city was as exquisite as ever under the deep yellow sun. The sky was cloudless and I began to relax, feeling that I could spend the rest of my life in Varnal and its surrounds. Here a dome caught the light and flashed brightly; there a little white house nestled between an impressive ziggurat on one side and a slender tower on the other. People moved about in a leisurely yet purposeful way. A fruit market was busy, but there was none of the noise and bustle of a similar Earthly market-place. As we rode around the city, Shizala told me much about it.

The Karnala as a race had always been primarily traders. Their origins were the same as many races— they had started off as barbarian raiders and finally settled on one part of the country they had liked. But instead of turning to farming they had continued to travel as traders instead of raiders. Because of daring expeditions to far parts of Vashu, they had become very rich, trading southern artifacts for northern precious metals, and so on.

The Karnala were also great artists, musicians and—what was highly worthwhile in terms of trade as well as everything else—the finest book producers in their world. The printing presses of Karnala, I learned, were of a flatbed type, not so fast as the rotary machines on Earth, but producing what appeared to my eye much sharper printing. The Sanskrit-like lettering I still could not read but, as Shizala took me round a small press, showing me some of the beautifully made books it produced, I soon learned to recognize many words as she pointed them out to me.

These books were in great demand across the whole continent and were a great asset to the Karnala, as were their artists and writers who produced the raw material.

Other industries thrived in Varnal. Their sword-smiths were also renowned throughout the world, I learned. The smiths still worked by the old methods, using furnace and anvil much as smiths on Earth worked—an earth that was yet to come, I realized.

Some farming was done now, but on a big scale and not by private landowners. Square miles of cereals were sown, I was told, and harvested all at once by volunteers from all over the Karnala nation. What was not used was stored in case of hard times, for the Karnala were well aware that a nation based on trade and industry cannot buy food in famine and will only survive if it can produce its own.

The absence of any places of worship was notice-able and I asked Shizala about this. She replied that there was no official religion of any kind, but for those who wanted to believe in a higher being it was better to look for Him in their own minds and hearts, not to seek Him in the words of others.

On the other hand, there were public schools, li-braries, clinics, social centers, hotels and the like, and no one seemed under-privileged or unhappy in Var-nal.

The Karnala political philosophy seemed to be one of armed neutrality. They were a strong nation and prepared for any attack. Besides this, an old-fashioned martial code still seemed to exist, because an aggressor never attacked without good warning.

After telling me this, Shizala added: "Apart from the more savage tribes, and they are no threat. Those—and the Blue Giants."

"Who are the Blue Giants?" I asked.

"The Argzoon. They are fierce and without code or conscience. They dwell in the far north and only venture out on raids. They have only once come this far south, and then my father's army drove them away . . ." She bowed her head and tightened her grip of the reins.

"And never returned?" I said sympathetically, feeling I had to say something.

"Just so."

She jostled the reins and the dahara began to trot faster. I imitated her and we were soon galloping along the wide streets through which the delicate green mist wound, and up towards the golden hills— the Calling Hills.

We were soon out of the city and rushing through the strange trees which seemed to be calling for us as we moved among them.

After a while Shizala slowed her steed and I did likewise. She turned to me with a smile.

"I acted wilfully—I hope you will forgive me."

"I could forgive you anything," I said, almost without thinking.

She gave me a quizzical, intelligent look which again I could not interpret.

"Perhaps," she said. "I should mention . . ."

Again I spoke on impulse. "Let us not talk—we are interrupting the voices of the trees. Let us just ride and listen."

She smiled. "Very well."

As we rode I suddenly began to wonder how I was

going to live on Mars. I had accepted that I would
like to stay in the idyllic city of Varnal—I would never
willingly leave a place which sheltered such a graceful
beauty as the girl riding beside me at that moment—
but how was I going to earn my living?

As a scientist I could probably contribute something to the industries. It struck me that Shizala might
be interested if I suggested that she elect me as some
sort of Court Scientific Adviser! This would allow me
to serve a useful function in the community and at the
same time enable me to be close to her and see a great
deal of her.

At that time, of course, I was acting almost intu-
itively. I had not as yet wondered if the customs of
the Karnala would even permit me to propose mar-
riage to Shizala—and, anyway, there was a very good
chance that Shizala would want nothing to do with
me. Why should she? Although she had not questioned what I had told her about where I had come
from and how I had arrived on her planet, for all she
knew I might be a lunatic.

My mind was confused as I rode along. At length
we decided we had best return to the city and the palace, and I directed my strange steed back with some
reluctance.

The visiting Prince of Mishim Tep, Telem Fas
Ogdai, was waiting on the steps of the palace when
we arrived. He had one foot on a higher step and his
hand rested on the hilt of his long, broadbladed
sword. He wore soft boots and a heavy cloak of dark
material. He looked both angry and impatient, and
twice as I dismounted and walked up the steps towards him, removed his hand from his sword-hilt to
finger the plain gold bangle on his wrist.

He ignored me but flashed a glance at Shizala and then turned his back on both of us, rumbling up the steps into the palace.

Shizala looked at me apologetically. "I am sorry, Michael Kane—but I had better speak to the Bradhinak. Will you excuse me? You will find food in the hall."

I bowed. "Of course. I hope to see you again later."

She gave me a quick, half-nervous smile and then she was tripping up the steps after Bradhinak.

Some diplomatic problem, I guessed, since the prince was evidently an emissary of some kind and was here on diplomatic business as well as a friendly visit.

Perhaps Karnala's strength had been sapped in the battle and the following expedition which had lost them their king. Perhaps they were forced to rely on stronger allies while they built up their strength again—and perhaps Mishim Tep was one of these allies. All this speculation seemed likely—and much of it was subsequently proved correct.

I entered the great hall. A kind off buffet meal had been laid out on the table by servants. Cold meat, fruit, the inevitable basu, sweetmeats and so forth. I sampled a little of everything and found almost all of it to my liking. I exchanged small talk with some of the men and women around the table. They were evidently very curious about me but too polite to ask too many direct questions—which I did not feel in any mood to answer at that moment.

As I munched on a particularly tasty piece of meat wrapped in a green, lettuce-like leaf, I suddenly heard an odd sound. I was not sure what it was, but I listened carefully so that I should hear it again if it came.

The courtiers had fallen silent and were also listening.

Then the sound came again.

A muffled cry.

The courtiers looked at one another in apparent consternation but made no move towards the source of the cry.

It came a third time and now I was sure I recognized the voice.

It was Shizala's!

Although there were guards at intervals around the hall, none of them moved and no orders were given to go to Shizala's assistance.

Desperately, I looked round at the courtiers. "That is your Bradhinaka's voice—why don't you help her? Where is she?"

One of the courtiers looked very disturbed and pointed to a door leading off the hall. "She is there—we cannot help her unless she summons us. It is a very delicate matter involving the Bradhinak Telem Fas Ogdai . . ."

"You mean he is causing her pain! I will not allow it. I thought you were people of character—but you just stand here . . ."

"I told you—the situation is delicate. We feel very deeply . . . But etiquette . . ."

"To hell with etiquette," I said in English. "This is no time for niceties—Shizala may be in danger."

And with that I strode towards the door he had pointed to. It was not locked and I flung it open.

Telem Fas Ogda was holding Shizala's wrists in a cruel grip and she was struggling. He was speaking to her in a low, urgent tone. When she saw me she gasped:

"No, Michael Kane—go from here. It will mean more trouble."

"I will not leave while I know this boor is troubling you," I said, flicking him a look of scorn.

He frowned, then he grinned evilly and his teeth flashed.

He still held her wrists.

"Let her go!" I warned, stepping forward.

"No, Michael Kane," she said. "Telem Fas Ogdai means me no harm. We are having an argument, that is all. It will end . . ."

But I had put my hand on the prince's shoulder now and I let it lie there heavily.

"Release her," I ordered.

He released her all right—and at the same time swung both his fists round to catch me on the head, sending me reeling. That was it! My temper got the better of me and I surged back in. A punch on the chest winded him and a following punch on the jaw knocked him back. He tried to retaliate so I punched him on the jaw again. He went down with a clatter and stayed down.

"Oh!" cried Shizala. "Michael Kane, what have you done?"

"I have dealt with a brute who was hurting a very beautiful and sweet young lady," I said, rubbing my fists. "I am sorry that it had to happen, but he deserved it."

"He has a bad temper sometimes, but he is not evil. I am sure you did what you thought was best, Michael Kane, but now you have made things even worse for me."

"If he is here on diplomatic business he should behave like a diplomat and with dignity," I reminded her.

"Diplomat? He is no emissary from Mishim Tep. He is my betrothed—did you not see the armlet on his wrist?"

"Armlet—so that's what it is! Your betrothed! But—but he can't be! Why would you consent to marry such a man?" I was horrified and bewildered. There was no chance of making her mine! "You could not love him!"

Now she frowned and it sent a shudder through me to see that I had angered her. She drew herself up and pulled a bell-cord. "You do not behave as befits a stranger and a guest," she said coldly. "You presume too much!"

"I am sorry—deeply sorry. I was impulsive. But . . ."

In the same emotionless voice, she said: "It was my father's wish that when he died and I succeeded him I should marry the son of his old ally, thus making sure of the Karnala's security. I intend to respect my father's wish. You are presumptuous to make any comment concerning my relationship with the Brad-hinak of Mishim Tep."

This was a side of Shizala I had not seen before—the regal side. I must have offended her deeply for her to adopt this manner and tone, for I knew it was not natural.

"I—I am very sorry."

"I accept your apology. You will not interfere again. Now, please leave."

In confusion, I turned and left the room.

Bewildered, I walked straight from the great hall,

down the steps of the palace to where a servant was just leading away the dahara I had been riding earlier.

With a muttered word to the servant I mounted the beast and shook its reins, making it gallop away down the main street towards one of the gates of the city.

I had to go right away from Varnal for the time being, had to go somewhere where I could be alone to collect my thoughts and pull myself together.

Shizala betrothed! A girl whom, I knew now, I had loved from the moment I saw her. It was too much to bear!

My heart beating much more rapidly than normal and my thoughts racing, my whole being seething with anguish, I rode blindly from the city, past the Green Lake and out into the Calling Hills.

Oh, Shizala, Shizala, I thought, I could have made you so happy.

I believe that I was close to crying then. I, Michael Kane, who had always prided himself on his self-control.

It was some time before I slowed my pace and began to make myself think levelly.

I did not know how far I had ridden. Many, many miles I suspected. My surroundings were unfamiliar. There was no landmarks I could recognize.

It was then that I saw a movement to the north. At first I thought I was looking at a distant herd of beasts galloping towards me but, shading my eyes from the sun, I soon realized that these were riders mounted on some sort of beast similar to my dahara. Many riders.

A horde!

Knowing so little of Martian geography or, for that

matter, politics, I did not know whether these riders threatened danger or not.

I sat my beast, watching them advance at a tremendous pace. Even so far away from them I could feel the ground faintly trembling, reverberating to the sound of the thundering animals.

Something seemed a little strange as they approached closer. I guessed they still could not see me—one solitary figure—but I could see them.

The scale was wrong. That was it.

Judging the average height of man and mount against the average height of trees and shrubs, I knew that these riders and their steeds were gigantic! Not one of their daharas was less than twice the height of mine; not one rider was under eight feet tall.

My memory worked swiftly and came up with only one answer.

These were invaders!

More—I thought I knew them.

They could only be those fierce, northern raiders Shizala had mentioned. *The Blue Giants—the Argzoon!*

Why had the city had no warning of the horde's approach?

How had they managed to come this far undetected?

These questions rose in my mind as I watched, but I dismissed them as useless. The fact was that a mounted force of warriors—thousands of them it seemed—were riding towards Varnal!

Quickly, I turned my beast, all thoughts of my grief now forgotten. I was obsessed by the emergency. I must warn the city. At least they would have a little time!

I checked my position from the sun and guided the swiftly-moving dahara back the way I had come.

But I had not reckoned with the Argzoon outriders. Though I had observed the main horde, the scouts sent ahead had evidently observed *me!*

As I ducked low to avoid the low branches of the slim trees and emerged into a wide glade, I heard a huge snort and a strange, wild, gusty laugh.

Then I was staring at a mounted giant towering above me on his great beast. In one hand he held an enormous sword and in the other an oval-headed mace of some kind.

I was unarmed—save for the slender lances that still reposed in the holster at my side.

CHAPTER FOUR

THE ATTACK

M Y mind raced. For a moment I felt completely overwhelmed, staring up into the face of a being that was to me as impossible as the unicorn or the hippogriff.

His skin was a dark, mottled blue. Like the folk of Varnal, he did not wear what we should think of as clothing. His body was a mass of padded leather armor and on his seemingly hairless head was a tough cap, also of padded leather, but reinforced with metal.

His face was broad yet tapering, with slitted eyes and a great gash of a mouth that was open now in laughing anticipation of my rapid demise. A mouth full of black teeth, uneven and jagged. The ears were pointed and large, sweeping back from the skull. The arms were bare, save for wristguards, and strongly muscled on a fantastic scale. The fingers were covered—encrusted would be a better description—with crudely-cut precious stones.

His dahara was not the quiet beast that I rode. It seemed as fierce as its rider, pawing at the delicate green moss of the glade, its head sporting a metal spike and its body partially protected by the same dark brown, padded leather armor.

The Argzoon warrior uttered a few guttural words which I could not understand, though they were clearly in the same language that I now spoke so fluently.

Fatalistically feeling that if I must die I would die fighting, I reached for one of the lances in the holster.

The warrior laughed again jeeringly and waved his sword, clapping his massive legs to his mount's side and goading it forward.

Now my reactions came to my rescue.

Swiftly, I plucked one of the lances from the holster and almost in the same motion got its balance, then flung it at the giant's face.

He roared as it hurtled towards him but with incredible speed for one so huge he struck it aside with his sword.

But by that time I had another lance in my hand and turned my jittery mount away as the warrior advanced, his sword swooping down towards me.

I ducked and felt it pass within an inch of my scalp.

Then he had thundered past, carried on by the weight of his own momentum. I wheeled my beast and flung another lance at him as he tried to turn his mount, which was evidently less well trained than mine.

The lance caught him in the arm.

He yelled in pain and rage and this time his speed was even faster as he bore down on me again.

I had only two lances left.

I flung the third as he came in with his sword held out in front of him, like a cavalryman on Earth might once have held his sword in a charge.

The third lance missed. But at least my second had wounded his mace-arm and I only had the sword to contend with; I could not duck this one. But what could I do? There were split seconds in which to decide!

Grabbing the remaining lance, I flung myself off the beast and fell to the ground just as the sword met air where I would have been.

Bruised, I picked myself up. I still gripped the last lance.

I would have to use it with certainty if I were to win this duel.

I crouched, waiting as he turned, poised on the balls of my feet, watching the gigantic, snorting brute as he fought his dahara, turning it round again.

Then he paused, laughing that gusty, animal laughter, his blue head flung back and his vast chest heaving beneath its armor.

It was his mistake.

Thanking providence for this opportunity, I hurled the lance with all my force and skill—straight at the momentarily exposed neck.

It went in some inches and for a brief instant the laughter still came from his mortally wounded throat. The noise changed to a shocked gurgle, a high sigh, and then my opponent pitched backward off his dahara and lay dead on the ground.

As soon as it was relieved of its ride, the dahara galloped away into the forest.

I was left, panting and dazed but grateful for the fortuitous opportunity I had been given. I should have been dead. Instead, I was alive—and still whole.

I had expected to die. I had not counted on the incredible stupidity of an adversary who had been so sure of victory he had exposed a vital spot which could only have been reached by the very weapon I happened to possess.

I stood over the great hulk. It lay spread out on the moss, the sword and mace still attached by wrist-thongs to its arms. There was a stink about it not of death but of general uncleanliness. The slitted eyes stared, the mouth still a grinning gash, though now it grinned in death.

I looked at his sword.

It was, of course, a great weapon, such as only a nine-foot giant would use. Yet, proportionately, it was almost a short sword—just over five feet long. Fastidiously I bent down and unhooked the thong from the creature's wrist. I picked the sword up. It was very heavy, but finely balanced. I could not use it in one hand as the Argzoon scout had done, but I could use it as a broadsword in two hands. The grips were just right. I hefted it, feeling better, thanking heaven for M. Clarchet, my old fencing master, who had taught me how to get the most out of any blade, no matter how strange or crude it at first seemed.

Holding it by its thong, I remounted my beast and lay the sword across my legs as I rode in that still peculiar riding position back towards the city.

There was a long way to go and I had to hurry—even more so now—to warn the city of the imminent attack.

But as I rode up hill and down dale for what seemed hours, I was to be threatened once again by an Argzoon giant who came riding at me from my right flank as I rode down one of the last hillsides before Varnal.

He did not laugh. Indeed, he uttered no sound at

all as he came at me. Evidently so near the city he did not wish to alert anyone who might be close by.

He had no mace—just a sword.

I met his first swing with my own recently acquired weapon. He looked at it in surprise, clearly recognizing it as one forged by his own folk.

His surprise served me well. These Argzoon were swift movers for their size, but poor thinkers—that had already been made quite plain.

While he was staring at my sword and at the same time bringing his own round for another blow, I did not swing up to protect myself but drove the sword towards where I hoped his heart would be. I also prayed it would pierce the armor.

It did, though not as swiftly as I had hoped and, as the blade struck through leather and then flesh, bone and sinew, his sword came down in a convulsive movement and grazed my right arm. It was not a bad wound but, within a moment, it was painful.

His sword dropped from inert fingers, dangling by its thong as he sat in his saddle, rocking dazedly and looking at me groggily.

I could see that he was badly wounded, though not mortally, I guessed.

As he began to topple from his saddle I reached out and tried to take his weight to stop him from falling. With my own wounded arm it was difficult, but I managed to hold him there while I inspected the injury I had inflicted.

Turned slightly by the padded armor, the sword had gone in just below the heart.

I managed somehow to dismount, still holding him, and lifted him down and laid him out on the moss.

He spoke to me then. He seemed very puzzled.

"What——?" he said in his thick, brutish accent.

"I am in a hurry. There, I have stopped the bleeding. It doesn't look fatal. Your own folk must look after you."

"You—you do not kill me?"

"It is not my way to kill if I do not have to!"

"But I have failed—the warriors of the Argzoon will torture me to death for that. Slay me, my vanquisher!"

"It is not my way," I insisted.

"Then . . ." He struggled up, reaching towards a knife in his belt. I forced the huge hand away and he sank back, exhausted.

"I will help you to that undergrowth." I pointed to some thick shrubbery nearby. "You can hide there and they will not find you."

I realized I was showing him more mercy than he expected, even from the folk of Varnal. And in helping him I was slowing myself up. Yet a man is a man, I thought—he cannot do what is contrary to his own feelings and principles. If he has a code of honor he must adhere to it. The moment he forgets that code, then all is lost, for even though he forgets on one occasion, it is the beginning of the end. Bit by bit the code will be qualified, any break with it justified, until the man is no longer a man, in truth, at all.

That is why I helped the odd being I had vanquished. I could do nothing less. As I had told him— it was my way. Such emotions may sound old-fashioned, even prudish, in this modern age where values are changing—many think for the worse—or things are losing their values altogether. But though I realize I may sound stiff and peculiar to many of my contemporaries, I am afraid that then, in that gentle valley on ancient Mars, just as now, on Earth, I had a set of principles—call it what you will—that I knew I must abide by.

As soon as I had hauled the creature to cover, I sent his dahara galloping away and mounted my own.

Within a few minutes I had reached the gates of the city and was riding desperately through them, shouting my warning.

"Attack! Attack! It is the hordes of Argzoon!"

The men looked startled but evidently they, too, recognized the type of sword I was carrying. The gates began to close behind me.

Straight to the palace steps I rode and flung myself from the exhausted dahara, running up the steps, half staggering with pain, exhaustion and the weight of the sword—proof of what I had to tell!

Shizala came running into the main hall. She looked disheveled and her face bore traces of her earlier anger.

"What is it? Michael Kane! What means this disturbance?"

"The Argzoon!" I blurted out "The Blue Giants— your enemies—a great horde of them attacks the city!"

"Impossible! Why have we not heard? We have our mirror posts that signal messages from hill to hill. We should have heard. Yet . . ."

She frowned thoughtfully.

"What is it?" I asked.

"The mirrors have had no messages for some time. Perhaps the stations were destroyed by the wily Argzoon."

"If they have reached this far before, they will have known roughly what to expect."

"But from where comes their strength! We had thought them beaten and quiescent for at least another ten years. They were all but wiped out by my father's army and its allies! My father headed the army which hunted down the survivors!"

"Well, the horde he defeated must have been only a fraction of the Argzoon strength. Perhaps this raid is part of a consistent strategy of surprise, meant to weaken you."

"If that is their plan," she sighed, squaring her beautiful creamy shoulders, "then it was a good one, for in truth we are unprepared!"

"No time for self-recrimination now," I pointed out. "Where is your brother Darnad? As chief Pukan-Nara of Varnal it is up to him to direct preparations for defense. What of the other warriors of Karnala?"

"They patrol borders, keep the peace against roaming bandit bands. Our army is scattered, but even if it were all assembled in Varnal it might not suffice to meet an Argzoon horde!"

"It seems impossible that you received no warning at all—not even a runner from another city. How have the Argzoon been able to get this far south without you knowing?"

"I cannot think. As you say, it could be that they have been planning this for years, that they have had spies not of their own race working for them, travelling in small groups under cover at night and in disguise, assembling in some nearby remote quarter of our land—and now ride on the city with none of our allies knowing our fate."

"The walls will resist heavy siege," I pointed out.

"You say you have some aircraft. You can bombard them from the air, using your Sheev-guns. That is one advantage."

"Our three aircraft will not achieve much against so large a force."

"Then you must send one of them to your nearest ally. Send your—your . . ." I paused as memory flooded back. "Send the Bradhinak of Mishim Tep to summon his father's aid—and seek help from your other, weaker, allies on the way."

She frowned thoughtfully and then looked up at me with a strange, half-puzzled look. She pursed her lips.

"I will do as you suggest," she said at length. "But even at their fastest our aircraft will take several days to reach Mishim Tep—and an army will take even longer getting here. We will have difficulty resisting so long a siege!"

"But outlast it and resist it we must—for Varnal and for the security of your neighboring states," I told her. "If the Argzoon conquer the Karnala, then they will sweep on across other nations. They must be stopped at Varnal—or your entire civilization could go under!"

"You have a clearer idea of what is at stake than I." She smiled slightly. "And you have only been with us a short time."

"Warfare," I said quietly, thinking of my own experiences, "does not seem to change much anywhere. The basic issues remain much the same—the strategy, the aims. I have already encountered two of your Blue Giants and hate to think of this lovely city being ruled by them!"

I did not add that it was not only the city I feared for but Shizala, too. Try as I might, I could not make myself forget the emotion I felt for her. I knew now she was betrothed to another and that whatever she or I felt it was impossible that anything could come of it. Evidently her code was quite as strong as mine and would not let her weaken, just as I did not intend to weaken.

For a long moment we looked into each other's eyes and all this was there—the pain, the knowledge, the resolution.

Or did I simply imagine that she was to some degree attracted to me? I must not think such thoughts, in any case. It was over—and Varnal must be protected.

"Have you more suitable arms for me than this?" I said, indicating the Argzoon sword.

"Of course. I will call a guard. He will take you to the arms room where you can select whatever weapons you wish."

At her command, one of the guards stepped forward and she ordered him to take me to the arms room.

He led me down several flights of steps until we were deeper below the palace than I had been before.

At last he stopped at two huge, metal-studded doors and cried:

"Guard of the Tenth Watch—it is Ino-Pukan Hara with the guest of the Bradhinak! Please open." An Ino-Pakan, I now knew, was a warrior with a rank about equivalent to sergeant.

The doors moved slowly open and I stood in a long hall of great size, dimly lit by the waning blue bulbs in the roof.

The guard who admitted us was an old man with

a long beard. At his belt were twin pistols. He carried no other weapons.

He looked at me quizzically.

The Ino-Pukan said: "The Bradhinaka wishes her guest to arm himself as he pleases. The Argzoon attack!"

"Again? But I thought them finished!"

"Not so," said the Ino-Pukan sadly. "According to our guest here, they are almost upon us."

"So the Bradhi died in vain—we are still to be vanquished." The old man's voice sounded hopeless as he let me wander up the hall admiring the great assortment of weapons.

"We are not defeated yet," I reminded him, staring at rack upon rack of fine swords. I took several down, testing them for length, weight and balance. At last I selected a long, fairly slim sword, rather like a straight sabre, with a blade as long as the sword I had taken from my Argzoon opponent.

It had a beautiful balance. It had a basket hilt and, as with swords on Earth of the same kind, one curled two fingers, the index and the one next to it, around the crosspiece, gripping it with the thumb along the top of the hilt with the remaining two fingers curled under. That may seem an awkward grip to some, but it is actually quite comfortable and also has the advantage of making sure that the sword is not easily knocked from the grasp.

I found a broad belt, equipped at the side with a wide sword-loop of leather. It seemed traditional in Varnal that swords were carried naked and not scabbarded—some old custom from less peaceful times internally, I gathered.

There were also guns that seemed operated by a

combination of spring and air. I took one of these
from its place and turned to the old keeper of the arms
room.

"Do many use these?" I asked.

"Some, our guest." He took the gun from my hand
and showed me how it loaded. A magazine of steel
darts was exposed. These, in the manner of airgun
darts, could be slid automatically into the breech. The
air was automatically repressured after a shot—this
was done by means of the spring attachment. A very
fine piece of craftsmanship but, as the old man demon-
strated, the accuracy was all but nil! The gun bucked
so much as it shot its missile that the target had to
be very close indeed if one was to have much success
in hitting him!

Still, my arms belt had a place for a gun—another
leather loop—so I slipped the airgun in. Now with the
gun and sword I felt better and was eager to rejoin
Shizala to see how the preparations were progressing.

I thanked the old man and, accompanied by the
Ino-Pukan, strode back up to the ground level of the
palace. Shizala was not in the hall, but another guard
led me up many flights of stairs that grew increasingly
narrower until we were standing outside a room that
obviously was in one of the circular towers rising from
the main building of the palace.

The guard knocked.

Shizala's voice called for us to enter.

We did so and Shizala stood there with Telem Fas
Ogdai and her brother, the Bradhinak Darnad.
Darnad darted me a quick smile of acknowledgment.
Shizala's welcome was a gracious movement of the
head, but Telem Fas Ogdai's smile was stiff and frosty.
He evidently had not forgotten our earlier encounter

that day. I couldn't blame him now, though I still disliked him greatly. I put my feelings about him down to the situation and made an effort to dismiss them as best I could.

Darnad had spread out a map. It was a little strange to me, this method of map-making. The symbols for cities, forests and so on were not pictorial as ours tend to be, but at last I had some idea of where we were in relation to the rest of that mighty continent—and to Mishim Tep and our other allies. I could also point out where I had seen the Argzoon and at what speed they had been travelling, and so on.

"Little time," Darnad murmured thoughtfully, running his fingers through his long, near-white hair. His other hand gripped his sword-hilt. He seemed very young just then—probably little more than seventeen. A boy playing at soldiers, one would have thought at first glance. Then I noted the look of responsibility he wore, the confident way he carried himself, the unself-conscious, unstudied mannerisms.

He began to speak rapidly to us, suggesting where the weakest points would be in the city walls and how they would best be defended.

Having had some training in warfare, I was able to make some suggestions which he found useful. He looked at me with something like admiration and I accepted the look as a compliment, for I might have been doing much the same. His essential manliness and clear-headed, objective attitude to the task ahead made me feel that he was ideal as a military leader, and I felt that to fight beside him would be reassuring, to say the least. It would also be, in its way, a pleasure.

Shizala turned to Telem Fas Ogdai.

"And now, Telem, you have seen what we shall try

to do and will have some idea of what our chances are of holding off the Argzoon. An aircraft awaits you at the hangars. Luckily, its motor has been prepared, since we planned to show it to our guest. Go swiftly and make sure that reinforcements are sent at once from all cities allied to Varnal. And tell them if Varnal falls, their chances of withstanding the Argzoon are lessened."

Telem bowed slightly, formally, looked deep into her eyes, darted me another of his looks and left the chamber.

We returned to the study of the map.

From the balcony of the tower it was possible to see the whole lovely city laid out beneath us—and we could see the surrounding countryside.

After a while we took the map out on to the balcony. It was as if we felt something was imminent—as, indeed, something was!

A short time later Darnad pointed.

"Telem leaves," he said to his sister.

Although there had been talk of aircraft I had not expected the sight which greeted me.

The aircraft was of metal, but it rose and navigated like an old fashioned airship—gracefully, slowly. It was oval in shape and had portholes dotted along its length. It gleamed like richly burnished gold and was heavily ornamented with pictures of strange beasts and symbols.

It swung in the air as if defying the very laws of gravity and then began to move towards the south, travelling rapidly by my standards, but with a stately dignity which could not be matched by any aircraft ever known to Earth.

It was not out of sight before Darnad pointed again—this time to our north-east.

"Look!"

"The Argzoon!" gasped Shizala.

The horde was coming. We could see the first wave clearly, looking like an army of marching ants from where we stood, yet the menace implicit in its steady progress could not be ignored. We all felt it.

"You did not exaggerate, Michael Kane," Darnad said softly. I could see his knuckles whiten on his sword-hilt.

The air was still and very faintly we could hear their shouts. Thin shouts now—but, having already had some experience of the sounds that the Argzoon warriors could make, I imagined what the noise must be like at the source!

Darnad stepped back into the room and came out on to the balcony again, clutching what was obviously a megaphone.

He leaned over the balcony, peering down into a courtyard where a group of guards stood ready.

He put the megaphone to his mouth and shouted to them.

"Commanders of the wall—to your posts. The Argzoon come." He then relayed specific orders based on what we had discussed a short time before.

As the commanders marched away to take charge of their men and position them, we watched in awful fascination as the horde approached.

Rapidly—too rapidly for us—they began to near the walls. We saw movement from within the city, saw warriors taking up their posts. They stood still, awaiting the first attack.

There were too few of them, I thought—far too few!

CHAPTER FIVE

A DESPERATE PLAN

A T least we held the wall against the first wave. The whole city seemed to shake at their onslaught. The air was ripped by their great, roaring shouts, polluted by the stink of their incendiary bombs launched from catapults, and by the odor of their very bodies. Flame licked here, crackled there—and the women and children of Varnal struggled valiantly to extinguish it. The sounds of clashing steel, of dying or victorious war-cries, the swish of missiles—blazing balls of some pitch-like substance—as they hurtled overhead and dropped in streets and on roofs.

Shizala and I still watched from the balcony but I felt impatient, anxious to join the brave warriors defending the city. Darnad had already gone to rally his men.

I turned to Shizala, feeling moved, in spite of myself, at her closeness. "What of your remaining aircraft? Where are they?"

"We are keeping them in reserve," she told me. "They will be of better use as a surprise later."

"I understand," I told her. "But what can I do? How can I help?"

"Help? It is not for you—a guest—to concern yourself with our problems. I was thoughtless—I should have sent you away with Telem Fas Ogdai."

"I am not a coward," I reminded her. "I am a skilled swordsman and have been shown great kindness and hospitality by you and your folk. I would regard it as an honor to fight for you!"

She smiled then. "You are a noble stranger, Michael Kane. I know not how you came to Vashu—but I feel it is good that you should be here now. Go then—find Darnad and he will tell you how you can help."

I bowed briefly and left, running down the stairs of the tower until I had reached the main hall, now in confusion, with men and women rushing this way and that.

I made my way through them, asking a warrior if he knew where I might find the Bradhinak Darnad.

"I heard that the east wall is weakest. You will probably find him there."

I thanked the warrior and left the palace, heading for the east wall. The main buildings of the city, sturdily built of stone as they were, were not damaged by the fire-bombs hurled by the Argzoon catapults, but here and there bundles of fabric and dry sticks had caught, and single pumps were being operated by women in an effort to put them out.

Thick smoke burnt my lungs and made my eyes water. My ears were assailed by cries and shouts from all sides.

And outside—outside the mighty hordes of Blue

Giants battered against the city walls. An invincible force?

I did not let my thoughts dwell on that idea!

At last I saw Darnad through the smoke near the wall. He was in consultation with two of his officers who were pointing up at the walls, evidently showing him the weakest points. He was frowning thoughtfully, his mouth set in a grim line.

"How can I assist you?" I asked, clapping him on the shoulder.

He looked up wearily.

"I do not know, Michael Kane. Could you magically bring half a million men to our aid?"

"No," I said, "but I can use a sword."

He deliberated. Plainly he was unsure of me and I could not blame him for wondering about one who was, after all, untried.

Just then there came an exultant shout from the wall—a shout that did not issue from a Karnala throat.

It was one of those roaring, triumphant shouts I had heard earlier.

All eyes turned upward.

"Zar! The devils have breached a section of our defense!"

We could see them. Only a few of the blue warriors had gained the top of the wall but, unless they were halted, I knew that soon hundreds would be stepping over.

Scarcely stopping to think, I drew my blade from my belt and leapt for the nearest ramp leading to the wall-top. I ran up it faster than I had ever thought possible.

A blue Argzoon warrior, towering above me, turned as I shouted a challenge from behind.

Again he voiced that deep, maniacal laugh. I lunged with my blade and he parried the thrust with a swift movement of his own thick sword. I danced and saw a slight chance as his arm came round. I darted my sword at the exposed upper arm and was fortunate enough to draw blood. He yelled an oath and swung at me with his other weapon, a short-hafted battle-axe. Again my faster speed saved me and I ducked in under his clumsy guard to take him high in the belly. The sword flashed into his flesh and came out again.

His eyes seemed to widen and then, with a dying growl, he toppled from the wall.

Another came at me, more cautiously than his comrade. Again I took the attack to the towering monster.

Twice I lunged, twice he parried, then he lunged at me. I blocked his thrust and saw that my blade was only an inch from his face. I pressed the blade forward and took him in the eye.

I had now got the feel of my sword—a marvellous weapon, better even than the best I had used on Earth.

Now reinforcements had come to my aid. I glanced down on the other side of the wall at what seemed to be a great tide of turbulent blue flesh, leathern armor and flashing steel. A scaling ladder had been raised. More of the Argzoon were scaling it.

That ladder had to be destroyed. I made it my objective.

Although the scene was so confused and I could hardly tell what the general situation was, I felt a peculiar calmness sweep over me.

I knew the feeling. I had experienced it before in

the jungles of Vietnam—had even experienced something like it in a particularly difficult engagement while fencing for sport.

Now that I had a few comrades at least, I felt even better. I stumbled on something and looked down. One of my assailants had lost his battle-axe. I picked it up in my left hand, testing its weight, and found it was not too badly balanced for me if I held it fairly close to the blade.

Both weapons ready, I moved forward in a half-crouched position towards the next blue invader.

He was leading his fellows along the wall towards the ramp. The wall was wide enough to take three of us, and two warriors ranged themselves on either side of me.

I felt rather like Horatius holding the bridge at that moment, but the Blue Giants were unlike Lars Porsena's men in that none of them was crying 'back.' They all seemed to have the same obsession—to press forward at all costs.

Their huge bodies came towards us, lumbering, powerful. Their slitted eyes stared black hatred at us and I shuddered as, for an instant, I stared directly into one face. There was something less than human, something primeval about that gaze—something so primitive that I felt I had a vision of Hell!

Then they were upon us!

I remember only a fury of fighting. The rapid cut and thrust of the duel; the desperate sense of *having* to hang on, *having* to win, *having* to bring out every ounce of energy and skill if we were to drive them back to the ladder—and destroy it.

Yet it seemed at first as if the most we could do was hold the wall against these huge beast-men looming above us with their great, corded muscles rolling under blue skins, their hate-filled, slitted eyes, their teeth-filled gashes of mouths, and their heavy weapons, the weight of which alone could sweep us from the wall to our doom!

I remember that my wrists, my arms, my back, my legs—my whole body—were aching. Then the aching seemed to stop and I felt only a strange numbness as we fought on.

I remember the killing, also.

We fought against their superior strength and numbers—and we killed. More than half-a-dozen Blue Giants fell beneath our blades.

We had more to fight for than just a city. We had an ideal, and this gave us a moral strength which the Argzoon lacked.

We began to advance, driving the giants back towards their ladder. This advantage gave us extra strength and we redoubled our attack, fighting shoulder to shoulder like old comrades—though I was a stranger from another planet, another time even.

And as the sun began to sink, staining the sky a deep purple shot with veins of scarlet and yellow, we had reached their ladder.

Holding the ladder we were able to stop the giants as they attempted to climb up.

While the others concentrated on stopping any more of the Argzoon gaining the wall, I chopped at the ladder as far down as I could, shortening it so that it no longer topped the wall. Spears clattered around me, but I worked on desperately.

At length my task was as finished as I could make it. I stood up, ignoring the missiles that flew about my body, took careful aim with the axe, aiming at the middle section of the ladder. Then I flung it.

It hit a main strut about half-way down and it went in deep. Several Argzoon warriors were above the place where I had hit the ladder. Their weight completed my work for me—the ladder cracked, splintered and then broke.

With horrible screams the Argzoon fell upon the heads of their comrades crowding the ground below.

Luckily it was the only ladder they had managed to raise, and only because the halberd-type weapons the defenders used to push the ladders back had not been available on this section.

This was rectified as two halberdiers took up their positions.

I was feeling somewhat shaky after my efforts and turned to grin at my comrades. One of them was a boy, even younger than Darnad—a redheaded youngster with freckles and a snub nose. I gripped his hand and shook it, though he was not familiar with the custom. Nonetheless, he responded in the right spirit, guessing the meaning of the gesture.

I reached out my hand to grasp that of the other man. He gave me a glazed look, tried to stretch out his own arm and then pitched forward towards me.

I knelt beside him and examined his wound. A blade had gone right through him. By rights he should have been dead an hour before. Head bowed, I paid my silent respects to such a brave fighter.

Then I was up again, looking around for Darnad, wondering how the battle went.

Night soon fell and flares were lighted.

It seemed we were to have some relief, for the Argzoon horde retreated some distance from the walls and began to pitch tents.

I staggered along the wall and down a ramp. I learned from a wall commander that Darnad had been called to the south wall but would be returning to the palace soon.

Rather than seek him along the wall, I went wearily back to the palace.

In the ante-room of the main hall, I found Shizala. The guard who had brought me here left and I was again uncomfortably alone with her. Even in my exhausted condition I could not help admiring her tall beauty.

At her silent indication I sank upon cushions that had been heaped on the floor.

She brought me a flask of basu. Thankfully I drank it down, almost in a single draught. Then I handed the flask back to her, feeling a little better.

"I have heard what you did," she said softly, not looking directly at me. "It was a heroic deed. Your action may have saved the city—or at least a large number of our warriors."

"It was necessary, that is all," I replied.

"You are a modest hero." She still did not look my way but raised her eyebrows a little ironically.

"Merely truthful," I replied in the same manner. "How goes the defense?"

She sighed. "Satisfactorily, considering our shortage of men and the size of the Argzoon horde. Those Argzoon, they are fighting well and cunningly—with more cunning than I had suspected they possessed. They must have a clever leader."

"I did not think cleverness was an Argzoon quality," I said, "from what I have experienced myself."

"Neither did I. If only we could reach their leader—to destroy him would probably defeat the entire plan of attack and the Argzoon, leaderless, might disperse."

"You think so?" I said.

"I think it likely. The Argzoon can rarely be persuaded to fight with overall strategy of the sort they are applying now. They pride themselves on their individuality—refuse to fight as an army or under any commander. They enjoy fighting, but not the discipline demanded for ambitious fighting involving armies and planned strategy. They must have a superior kind of leader if he has persuaded them to fight as they are doing now."

"How could we reach the leader?" I enquired. "We cannot disguise ourselves as Argzoon—we could dye ourselves blue but could not add eight or ten *kilodas* to our height"—a *kiloda* is about a third of a foot—"so an attempt to reach his tent would be impossible."

"Yes." She spoke tiredly.

"Unless"—a thought had suddenly struck me—"unless we could attack him from the air!"

"The air—yes . . ." Her eyes gleamed. "But even then we do not know who their leader is. They seem to be one great tide of warriors—I saw no obvious commanders. Did you?"

I shook my head. "And yet he must be out there somewhere. It was too confused today. Let us wait until dawn, when we will be able to see their camp before they resume the attack."

"Very well. You had better go to your room and sleep now—you have exhausted yourself and will need all your strength for tomorrow. I will have a guard wake you just before dawn."

I got up, bowed and left her. I went up to my room and stood for a moment at the window. The sweet smell of the Martian night—cool, somehow nostalgic—was tinged now by the stink of war.

How I hated those Blue Giants!

Someone had left some meat and fruit on the table next to my bed. I did not feel hungry but common sense told me to eat. I did. I washed the dried blood, dirt, and sweat of the day's warfare from me, climbed beneath that heavy fur and was asleep immediately I lay down.

Next morning the same girl servant awakened me. I received glances from her which were even more overtly admiring than before. It seemed I was something of a talking point in Varnal. I felt flattered but a little bewildered. After all, I had only done what anyone else would have done. I knew I had done my chosen task well, but that was all. I felt myself grow a trifle red with embarrassment as I accepted the food she brought me.

It was not yet dawn, but would be in a very short time—less than two *shatis,* I guessed. A *shati* is roughly an eighth of an Earth hour.

Just as I was buckling on my sword-belt, a light knock sounded on the door. I opened it and faced a guard.

"The Bradhinaka awaits you in the tower," he told me.

I thanked him and made my way up to the tower-chamber where we had met the previous day.

Shizala and Darnad were both there, already on the balcony, tense and waiting for the sun to rise.

It began to rise as I joined them. They said nothing as we exchanged nods.

Soon the sun was flooding golden light over the scene. It struck the lovely walls of Varnal, gleamed on water and illuminated the dark camp of the Argzoon surrounding our city. I say 'our' city because that is how I was already thinking of it—more so now.

The Argzoon tents were affairs of skin stretched on wooden frames—oval in shape mainly, though a few were circular or even square. Most of the common warriors seemed to be sleeping on the ground and were beginning to stir as light pervaded the scene.

But from one tent—no larger than the others—a banner flew. All the others were undecorated and tended to surround that solitary oval tent sitting in their centre. There was no doubt in my mind that the cunning Argzoon leader slept there.

"So now we know where their leader is," I said, staring hard at the waving Argzoon banner. It seemed to depict some sort of writhing, snake-like creature with eyes not unlike those of the Argzoon themselves.

"The N'aal Beast," Shizala explained with a shudder when I asked her what it symbolized. "Yes, it is the N'aal Beast."

"What—?" I broke off as Darnad pointed.

"Look," he cried, "they are already preparing to attack!"

He rushed back into the room and came out bearing a long, curling trumpet. He blew on this with all his might and a high, melancholy note echoed through the city. Other trumpet-calls sounded in reply.

The warriors of Varnal—many of whom had slept at their posts—began to make ready for another day's fighting. It could well be their last.

Shizala said: "Although it will take Telem Fas Ogdai another day before he reaches Mishim Tep, he

will have stopped off at nearer cities on the way and
relief might come by tonight or tomorrow morning.
If we can hold out until then . . ."

"We may not need to if I can borrow one of your
aircraft," I said. "It only needs one man to drop from
the air on to the Argzoon commander—and despatch
him."

She smiled. "You are very brave. But the aircraft
motors take the best part of a day to warm up. Even
if we switched them on now they would not be ready
before evening."

"Then I suggest that you order them to be switched
on at once," I said disappointedly, "for the opportunity might still arise and be welcomed by you when
it does."

"I will do as you say. But you would perish in a
venture such as you contemplate."

"It would be worth it," I said simply.

She turned away from me then, and I wondered
why. Perhaps she thought me stupid—an unintelli-
gent boor who only knew how to die. After all, I had
offended her earlier by behaving tactlessly and unsub-
tly. Again I controlled my thoughts. It did not matter
what she thought, I told myself.

I sighed. Knowing nothing of the science that had
developed the aircraft, I could not suggest any way
of getting their motors ready faster. Obviously, I
thought, it was some sort of slow reaction system—
probably very safe and foolproof, but at a time like
this I would have preferred something faster even if
more dangerous.

I felt as if Shizala were deliberately hampering me
for some reason, as if she did not want me to put my
plan into operation. I wondered why.

Darnad now put down the trumpet and clapped me on the shoulder. "Do you want to come with me?"

"Willingly," I said. "You must tell me how I can be most useful."

"I was unsure of you yesterday," he said with a smile. "But that is not true today."

"I'm glad. Farewell, Shizala."

"Farewell, sister," said Darnad.

She replied to neither of us as we left. I wondered if I had offended her in some way. After all, I was unfamiliar with the customs of Vashu and might have done so unknowingly.

But there was no time for such speculation.

Soon the walls of the city were shaking again to another Argzoon attack. I helped with the siege weapons, tipping cylinders of flaring fat down on the attackers, hurling stones on them, flinging their own javelins back into their ranks.

They seemed to care little for their own lives and even less for the lives of their comrades. As Shizala had pointed out, they were individualistic warriors and, though they were taking part in an organized mass attack, you could still see that they were having to control their own instincts. Once or twice I saw a couple of them fighting between themselves while their fellows milled around them and our missiles rained down.

By midday little had been gained or lost, save that whilst the defenders were weary almost to the point of dropping, the attackers could bring in fresh reserves. I learned that the system of reserves was alien to the Argzoon normally, and this was another puzzling factor of their attack.

Though fierce and feared, the Argzoon had never

been a really important threat since they could not be organized into one mass for long enough. Also, this monstrous attack so far from their homeland—an attack without warning—spoke of fantastic planning and ingenuity. It might also speak of treachery, I thought privately—an ally letting the horde through his land by pretending to ignore it. But I still did not know enough of Vashu politics to make any fair guesses.

In the afternoon I helped the members of an engineering squad force up special barriers in places where the wall had been badly weakened by Argzoon rams and catapults.

Turning and wiping sweat from my brow after a particularly difficult piece of manipulating, I discovered Shizala at my side.

"You seem able to turn your hand to anything." She smiled.

"The test of a good scientist—the test of a good soldier," I replied, returning her smile.

"I suppose it is."

"How is the aircraft coming along?"

"It will be ready just before dusk."

"Good."

"You are sure you want to make the attempt?"

"Certain."

"You will need a specially trained pilot."

"Then I hope you'll supply one."

She dropped her gaze. "That will be arranged."

"Meanwhile," I said, "have you stopped to think that the Argzoon may have been able to arrive undetected here through the connivance of one of your 'allies'?"

"Impossible. None of our allies would stoop to such treachery."

"Forgive me," I said, "but though I am impressed by the code of honor possessed by the Karnala, I am not sure that all the races of Vashu possess it—particularly since I have seen another Vashuvian race almost as unlike the Karnala as it could possibly be."

She pursed her lips. "You must be wrong."

"Perhaps. But my explanation seems the likeliest. What if Mishim Tep were . . . ?"

Her eyes blazed. "So that is the foundation of your suspicion—jealousy of Telem Fas Ogdai! Well, let me point out that the Bradhi of Mishim Tep is my father's oldest friend and ally. They have fought many a battle together. The bonds of mutual help that exist between the two nations are centuries old. What you suggest is not only impertinent—it is base!"

"I was only going to say . . ."

"Say no more, Michael Kane!" She turned on her heel and left.

I may tell you, I had little stomach for further fighting just then.

Yet, scarcely three *shatis* later, I was part of a small body of warriors defending a breach that the Argzoon had made in the wall.

Steel clashed, blood spilled, the stench of death was everywhere. We stood on the broken masonry and fought off ten times our number of Blue Giants. Brave and ferocious as they were, the Blue Giants lacked our intelligence and speed—as well as our burning ideal to hold the city at all costs. These three advantages just seemed to balance the savage attacks which we somehow managed to withstand.

At one time I was engaging an Argzoon even larger

than most of his kind. Around his huge throat he wore a necklace of human bones and his helmet seemed constructed of several large, wildbeast skulls. He was evidently some sort of local commander.

He carried two large swords, one in each hand, and he whirled them before him so that facing him was rather like facing a propeller-driven plane!

I stumbled before the force of his attack and my foot slipped on a blood-wet stone. I fell backwards and lay there while, grinning jubilantly, he prepared to finish me.

He raised both swords to hack at my prone figure, and then somehow I swivelled my body and cut at his calves, deliberately slashing at the muscles just behind his knees.

One leg bent and he opened his mouth wide in a great roar of pain. Then the other leg bent and suddenly he was falling towards me.

Hastily I scrambled up and flung myself out of his path. With a tremendous crash he fell to the broken stones and I turned and finished him with a single sword-thrust.

Luck, providence—perhaps justice—were on our side that day. I cannot explain how else we managed to hold the city against the invaders.

But we did. Then, just four *shatis* before sunset, I left the wall and headed for the aircraft hangars that had been pointed out to me the day before.

The hangars were domed buildings near the central square of the city. There were three of them, side by side. The domes were not of stone, but of some metallic substance, another alloy with which I was unfamiliar.

The entrances were small, barely wide enough or

high enough for a man of my size to squeeze through. I thought this strange, and wondered how the aircraft could get out.

Shizala was in the first hangar I tried, supervising some male servants who were swinging one of the heavy aircraft round on davits. It was cradled in the davits, which swung slightly as they moved it.

The strange oval ship was even more beautiful at close view. It was evidently incredibly ancient. There was the aura of millennia of existence about it. I looked at it in fascination.

Shizala, tight-lipped, did not welcome me as I entered.

I gave her a slight bow, feeling uncomfortable.

A low thrum of power came from the ship. It looked more like a piece of sculpture in bronze-like substance than a vehicle. The complicated, raised designs spoke of a creative intelligence superior to any in my experience.

A simple rope-ladder led to the entrance. I walked up to this in silence and tested it.

I darted a look of enquiry at Shizalá.

At first she refused to meet my glance, but at length she did and said with a gesture at the ship: "Go aboard. Your pilot will join you in a moment."

"There is not much time," I reminded her. "This should be accomplished before nightfall."

"I am aware of that," she replied coldly.

I began to climb the swaying ladder, reached the top and entered the ship.

It was richly furnished, with padded couches of some deep green and gold material. At the far end were controls, as beautifully made and as finely decorated as the rest of the ship, with levers of brass—perhaps even gold—instruments encased in crystal. There was a small screen in a cabinet—some kind of television equipment which gave a wider view of what lay outside the ship than could be obtained through one of the rather small portholes.

After inspecting the interior of the ship I sat on one of the couches to work out my plan of assassination— for that, in essence, was what it was—and wait impatiently for my pilot to join me.

In a while I heard him climbing the rope-ladder. My back was to the entrance so I did not see him as he entered.

"Hurry," I said. "We have very little time!"

"I am aware of that," came Shizala's voice as she walked towards the controls and seated herself at them!

"Shizala! This is dangerous! It is no job for a woman!"

"No? Then who else do you suggest? Only a few pilots exist for the ships—and I am the only one available."

I was not sure that she spoke the truth, but there was no time to waste.

"Then be very careful," I said. "Your people need you more than I do—do not forget your responsibility to them."

"That I could never do," she said. For some reason I thought she spoke bitterly, though I could not determine why at that time.

Now she operated the controls and the ship began to rise, light as a feather, towards the roof. As the roof slid open, I realized how the ships left the hangars. The dark blue sky of late evening was above us. The ship's motors began to murmur with greater intensity.

Soon we were winging over the city towards the camp of the Argzoon. We noticed that they were beginning to retreat again, as was their night-time custom.

Our plan was simple. The ship would swoop down over the tent of the Argzoon commander. I would drop swiftly down the rope ladder. The oval tent had holes at the top, covered with thin gauze—presumably for better ventilation. The hole would just take a man. I had to drop through it and thus surprise the commander, engage him quickly and despatch him with expediency.

A simple plan—but one that would require swift reactions, excellent timing, and absolute accuracy.

As we began to move over the enemy camp, their great catapults sent huge stones hurtling into the air towards us. We had expected this. But we had also expected what happened next—the falling stones, of course, landed back in the Argzoon camp and the warriors naturally objected to being crushed by the artillery of their own forces. Soon the barrage ceased.

Within a short time our objective was reached.

At a signal from Shizala, I went to the entrance and began to pay out more of the rope-ladder from the drum near the door.

I darted a glance at her but she did not turn to look at me. I gazed down. I could see the Banner of the N'aal Beast stirring in the faint breeze that was beginning to blow.

The faces of hundreds of Argzoon were watching me, of course, for they had expected some sort of attack from us. I hoped they didn't realize what form it would take.

Looking down at them, I felt like a fly dropping into

a nest of giant spiders. I gathered my courage, made sure of my sword, drawing it in a single gesture, shouted once to Shizala and swung down the rope-ladder until I was directly over the gauze-covered opening of the leader's tent.

Argzoon were shouting and milling about. Several spears flashed past me. More then ten feet over the opening I decided it was now or never.

I let myself go and dropped towards the tent.

CHAPTER SIX

SALVATION—AND DISASTER!

THERE was a momentary roaring in my ears and then I was plummeting through the opening, dragging the gauze cover with me.

I landed on my feet but staggered as the air was forced from my lungs. Then I whirled to confront the occupants of the tent.

There were two of them—a large, battered Argzoon warrior, resplendent in rudely-beaten bangles and rough-hewn gems—and a woman! She was black-haired, dark-complexioned and had a haughty bearing. She was wrapped in a thick, black cloak of some velvet-like material. She stared at me in surprise. She was as far as I could tell an ordinary human woman! What was she doing here?

Outside came yells from the Argzoon warriors.

Ignoring the woman, I gestured to the battered Argzoon to draw his sword. He did so with a sharp grin and came at me suddenly.

He was an excellent swordsman and, still recovering from my drop into his tent, I was forced to fight a defensive duel for a few moments.

I had little time to do what I had come to accomplish. I met his thrusts with the fastest parries I have ever made, returned them with thrusts and lunges of my own. Our swords crossed perhaps a score of times before I saw a break in his guard and moved in swiftly, catching him in the heart and running him through.

At that moment several more Argzoon rushed into the tent. I turned to meet them but before we could engage the woman cried imperiously:

"Enough! Do not kill him yet. I wish to question him."

I remained on guard, suspecting a ruse of some sort, but the warriors seemed to be in the habit of obeying the woman's orders. They stood their ground.

Cautiously I turned to look at her. She was exotically beautiful in her wild, dark way, and her eyes smouldered mockingly.

"You are not of the Karnala," she said.

"How do you know that?"

"Your skin is the wrong texture, your hair is short—there is something about the set of your shoulders. I have never seen a man like you. Where are you from?"

"You would not believe me if I told you."

"Tell me!" She spoke fiercely.

I shrugged. "I come from Negalu," I said, using the Martian name for Earth.

"That is impossible. There are no men on Negalu."

"Not now. There will be."

She frowned. "You seem to speak truthfully but in some sort of riddle. You are perhaps a—a . . ." She seemed to regret what she was about to say, and stopped.

"A what?"

"What do you know of Raharumara?"

"Nothing."

This seemed to satisfy her. She put her knuckles to her mouth and seemed to gnaw them. Suddenly she looked up at me again.

"If you are not of the Karnala, why do you fight with them? Why did you jump into this tent and kill Ranak Mard?" She indicated the fallen Argzoon.

"Why do you think?"

She shook her head. "Why risk your life just to kill one Argzoon captain?"

"Is that all I did?"

She smiled suddenly. "Aha! I think I know. Yes, that is all you did."

My spirits sank. So I had been wrong. The tent did not hold some great Argzoon battle-leader. Perhaps it was a deliberate blind and the leader was elsewhere.

"What of you?" I said. "Are you a prisoner of these folk—a prisoner with some power?"

"Call me a prisoner if you like. I am Horguhl of the Vladnyar nation."

"Where lies Vladnyar?"

"You do not know? It lies to the north of Karnala, beyond Narvaash. The Vladnyar are ancient enemies of the Karnala."

"So Vladnyar has struck up an alliance with Argzoon?"

"Think what you like." She smiled secretively. "And now, I think, you will d——" She broke off as there came a great sound of fighting outside the tent. "What is that?"

I could not think. It was impossible that the small force of Karnala warriors in the city had attacked the Argzoon—that would have been folly. But what else?

As Horguhl and the Blue Giants turned towards

the sound, I seized my opportunity, stepped forward and ran one of the Argzoon through the throat. I fought my way through the others and found myself outside the tent, staring into the darkness as the remaining warriors came after me.

I ran in the general direction of the noise of battle. I darted a quick glance back above the tent, looking to see if Shizala had made good her escape.

The ship was still there—hovering above the tent!

Why hadn't she left? I stopped, uncertain what to do, and in a second found myself engaging several of the gigantic warriors. It was all I could do to protect my own life, but as I fought I got the impression that something was happening close by and suddenly, out of the corner of my eye, I saw a group of splendidly-armored warriors of about my own height break through a mass of blue swordsmen.

The warriors were not from the city, that was plain. They wore helmets, for one thing—helmets from which nodded brightly-colored plumes. Phobos and Deimos, coursing across the heavens, gave illumination to the scene around me. The new warriors also had lances and some carried what looked like metal crossbows.

Soon their foreguard had pressed forward until I found myself with several allies helping me to engage the Argzoon who were attacking me.

"Greetings, friend," said one of them in an accent only slightly different from the one I was familiar with.

"Greetings. Your presence here has saved my life," I replied in relieved gratitude. "Who are you?"

"We are from Srinai."

"Did Telem Fas Ogdai send you here?"

"No." The man's voice sounded a trifle surprised. "We were originally on our way to deal with a large force of bandits who fled into Karnala. That is why there are so many of us. A detachment of your border patrol were about to help us when a messenger came with news that the Argzoon were attacking Varnal— so we left the bandits and rode to Varnal as fast as we could."

"I am glad you did. What do you think our chances are of defeating them?"

"I doubt that we can—not completely. But we might be able to drive them away from Varnal and give your reinforcements time to come to your aid."

This conversation was carried on while fighting Argzoon warriors. But the Argzoon were becoming increasingly few and it seemed we were winning in that particular area, anyway.

At last we had them on the run and the combined force of Srinai and Karnala chased the retreating Argzoon towards the Calling Hills from whence they had come.

The Argzoon stood their ground on the crest of the first range of hills, and then we withdrew to count our strength and plan fresh strategy.

It was soon obvious that the Argzoon still outnumbered us and that the Srinai and Karnala who had attacked them from behind had had the advantage of being fresh and able to take the Argzoon by surprise.

But I felt much better. Now, I decided, we could withstand the next attack and hold the Argzoon off until help came.

Then I remembered the ship and Shizala. I returned to the now ruined Argzoon camp. The tent with the banner was still standing, unlike most of the others

and, rather strangely, the ship still hovered above it.
It seemed to me, peering through the moonlit darkness, that the ship was now lower above the roof, the
rope-ladder brushing the top of the tent.

I called her name, but silence greeted me. With a
feeling of foreboding I climbed up the yielding sides
of the tent. It was a hard climb, but I made it rapidly,
almost in panic. Sure enough, the rope-ladder was
closer, the ship lower. I grabbed the ladder and began
to clamber up it.

Soon I was inside the ship.

A brief glance showed me that it was empty.

Shizala had gone!

How? Where?

What had happened to her? What had she done?
Why had she left the slip? What reason was there for
doing such a thing?

All these thoughts raced through my brain and
then I was dropping down the rope-ladder again,
hand over hand, until I was above the now uncovered
roof-opening. I dropped through it as I had done earlier.

Save for the corpse of Ranak Mard the tent was
empty. Yet there were signs of a struggle and I noticed
that Ranak Mard's sword had been removed from his
dead grasp and now lay on the other side of the tent.

Something else lay beside it.

A gun.

A gun of the Sheev.

It could only be Shizala's gun.

The mysterious, dark-haired woman Horguhl and
the Argzoon warriors must have taken part in a struggle soon after I had left.

For some reason best known to herself, Shizala had

decided to follow me into the tent. She had found me gone, of course, and confronted Horguhl and the Argzoon. There had probably been a fight and Shizala had been overpowered and captured. She had not been killed—that was a mercy—or I should have found her corpse.

Abducted, then?

My misguided plan to kill the absent mastermind behind the Argzoon had been worthless. All my plan had succeeded in doing was putting a hostage in the hands of the Argzoon.

The best hostage they could ever hope for.

The ruler of Varnal.

I began to curse myself as I would never curse another, even my greatest enemy.

CHAPTER SEVEN

THE PURSUIT

THEN I was running from the tent, blind with remorse and anger. I rushed through the corpse-strewn field towards the Calling Hills, bent on Shizala's rescue!

I ran past startled warriors of the Srinai and the Karnala, who called after me enquiringly.

I began to run up the hill towards the spot where the Argzoon had taken their stand.

I heard more shouts behind me, the sound of fast-moving feet. I refused to pay them any attention.

Ahead and above, the Argzoon stirred, evidently thinking that we were launching another surprise attack on them.

Instead of holding their ground as I expected, they began to turn and run in twos and threes.

I yelled at them to stop and fight. I called them cowards.

They did not stop.

Soon it seemed that the whole Argzoon force was in full flight—pursued by one man with a sword!

Suddenly I felt something grapple my legs. I turned to meet this new adversary, wondering where he had come from. I raised my sword, striving to keep my balance.

More men jumped on me. I growled in fury, trying to fight them off. Then my head cleared for a moment and I realized that the one who had grappled me was none other than Darnad—Shizala's brother!

I could not understand why *he* should be attacking me. I cried out:

"Darnad—it is Michael Kane. Shizala—Shizala—they have . . ." Then came a blow on my head and I knew no more.

I awoke with a throbbing headache. I was in my room in the palace at Varnal. That much I could understand. But why?

Why had Darnad attacked me?

I fought to think clearly. I sat up rubbing my head.

The door suddenly opened and my attacker entered looking worried.

"Darnad! Why did you—?"

"How do you feel?"

"Worse than I would if your comrade had not knocked me out. Don't you realize that . . ."

"You are still excited, I see. We had to stop you, even though your madness resulted in the Argzoon fleeing in complete disorganization. As far as we can tell, they are now scattered. Your plan to slay their leader must have worked. They seem to have broken up completely. They no longer represent a threat to Varnal."

"But I slew the wrong man. I—" I paused. "What do you mean, my *madness*?"

"It sometimes happens that a warrior who has fought long and hard, as you did, is gripped by a kind of battle-rage in which—no matter how tired he might

be—he cannot stop fighting. We thought this was
what happened to you. There is another thing that
concerns me. Shizala—"

"Don't you realize what you have done?" I spoke
in a low, angry voice. "You speak of Shizala. Is she
here? Is she safe?"

"No—we cannot find her. She piloted the ship that
took you to the Argzoon camp, but the ship was
empty when we recovered it. We think that . . ."

"I *know* what has happened to her!"

"You know? Then why did you not tell us? Why—?"

"I was seized by no battle-rage, Darnad. I discovered that Shizala had been abducted. I was on my way
to try to rescue her when you set upon me. How long
ago was this?"

"Last night—about thirty-six shatis ago."

"Thirty-six!" I got up, giving an involuntary groan.
Not only my head ached. The exertions of the previous two days had taken their toll of my body. It
seemed a mass of bruises and minor wounds. My
worst wound—the one on my arm—was throbbing
painfully. Thirty-six shatis—more than four hours
ago!

As quickly as I could, I told Darnad all the details
of what I had learned. He was as surprised as I had
been to learn of Horguhl the Vladnyar woman.

"I wonder what part she plays in this?" he said with
a frown.

"I have no idea. Her answers were ambiguous, to
say the least."

"I am sorry that I made that mistake, Michael
Kane," he said. "I was a fool. I heard you shouting
something. I should have listened. With luck we
should have rescued Shizala and all would be over.

The Argzoon are scattered. We and our allies will soon have cleansed Karnala of them. We will be able to question prisoners and discover how they managed to reach Varnal undetected."

"But while we are doing this Shizala could be taken anywhere! North—south—east—west. How are you to know where they will carry her?"

Darnad dropped his eyes and stared at the floor.

"You are right. But if you think Shizala is with this Vladnyar girl, then we must hope that some of our prisoners will have seen which way they went. There is also the chance that in our general routing and capturing of the Argzoon we will manage to rescue Shizala."

"There is no time for recriminations of any kind," I said. "So let us forget the errors of judgment we have both made. The heat of the battle must be held to account. What do you intend to do now?"

"I shall be leading a force with the specific intention of capturing Argzoon and questioning them on the whereabouts of Shizala."

"Then I shall accompany you," I told him.

"That is what I hoped you would say," he said, patting my shoulder. "Rest while the last preparations are being made. I will call for you when we are ready to leave—there is nothing else you can do until then, and you had better regain as much strength as possible—you are going to need it. I will have food sent."

"Thank you," I said gratefully. He was right. I must make myself relax—for Shizala's sake.

As I lay back on the couch, I again wondered just why she had risked such danger by going into the Argzoon tent. There had been no need for it—and as ruler of her folk she should have returned at once to Varnal.

I decided that the sooner we found her the sooner we should have answers to these and other questions.

I slept until a servant entered with food. Then I ate the food and, on receiving a message that Darnad and his warriors were ready, washed hastily and went down to join them.

The day should have been grim and stark and full of storm-clouds. It was not. It was a lovely, clear day with the pale sun brightening the streets of the city and obscuring most traces of the strife that had so recently ended.

At the foot of the palace steps was a company of warriors mounted on dahara. Darnad was at their head, holding the reins of a dahara that was evidently meant for me.

I mounted the beast, stretching my legs out along it. Then the whole company turned into the street leading towards the main gate.

We were soon riding across the Calling Hills, tracking our fleeing enemy.

It was still a mystery why the Argzoon had fled so precipitately—particularly in the face of such a small force.

But we did not ask ourselves these questions as we rode grimly after our quarry, even though it seemed that Ranak Mard had, indeed, been the master-mind behind the Argzoon attack—for it was plain that he was dead and the Argzoon were now in confusion.

Yet why had Horguhl told me otherwise?

No questions. Not yet.

Find the Argzoon—they will answer our questions.

On we rode.

It was not until late in the afternoon that we managed to surprise a group of some ten weary Argzoon who had camped in a shallow valley far, far from the Calling Hills.

They rose up at our approach and stood ready to fight. For once *we* outnumbered *them*. Normally, this would not please me but I felt that in this case it made a pleasant change to have the advantage over the Argzoon.

They put up a token fight as we attacked them. About half were killed and then the others lay down their arms.

The Argzoon have no code of loyalty such as we understand it, and little sense of comradeship with one another. This made it easier to question them in one way—but harder in another.

They did not stay silent because they did not wish to betray their fellows. They stayed silent out of stubbornness.

It was not until Darnad significantly fingered his long dagger and hinted that, since they were no use to us, it would be as well to dispose of the Argzoon, that one of them broke.

We were lucky. He knew a great deal more than we had expected one simple warrior to know.

They had not crossed from Argzoon to Karnala by land at all but had spent over a year travelling by sea and river. They had gone round the coast, thousands of miles out of their way—for Varnal lay many thousands of miles inland—and then sailed down the Haal River, the largest of the rivers on the continent. They had assembled in a place called the Crimson Plain and then gone in small groups from there, moving at night all the time, until they reached Karnala undetected. We learned that one or two parties of Karnala war-

riors had discovered detachments of Argzoon, but the
Karnala had been wiped out.

"Simple," Darnad mused after hearing this. "And
yet we never credited the Argzoon with such ingenuity or patience. It just isn't in their nature to spend
so much time and thought on a raid. It is good that
you slew Ranak Mard, Michael Kane. He must have
been a strange sort of Argzoon."

"Now," I said, "let us try to discover where Shizala
has been taken."

But the Argzoon could not help beyond telling us
that as far as he knew all the Argzoon were fleeing
north. It seemed instinctive for them to go north, back
to their mountains, in defeat.

"I think he is right," said Darnad. "Our best
chance would be to try the north."

"North," I said—"that takes in a lot of territory."

Darnad sighed.

"True—but . . ." He looked at me directly and there
was a misery in his eyes that was only half hidden.

I reached out and grasped his shoulder. "But all we
can do is search on," I said. "We will make more prisoners soon and with luck we shall be able to get a better indication of where they have taken Shizala."

Our prisoners were tied securely and one of our
number undertook to escort them back to Varnal.

Now we rode across a vast plateau of short, waving
crimson fern. It was the Crimson Plain. It was like
a great sea of bright blood, stretching in all directions,
and I began to feel hopeless of ever finding Shizala.

Night fell and we camped, building no fires for fear
of ambush from Argzoon or from the marauding bandits who apparently roamed these plains, nomadic
bands made up from the riff-raff of all the nearby na-

tions. The Crimson Plain was a kind of no-man's land hardly touched by law of any sort—save the savage dog-eat-dog, weakest-to-the-wall law of the lawless.

I slept little. I was beginning to feel frustrated, wanting to find more Argzoon to question.

We moved off early, almost before dawn. It was no longer fine and the sky was full of grey clouds, a light drizzle falling.

We saw nothing of bandits or Argzoon until the next afternoon when suddenly in front of us some fifty Blue Giants rose up in our path. They looked ready for a fight—ready for vengeance on us for their defeat!

We scarcely paused as we drew lances and swords and goaded our mounts towards them, yelling as fiercely as they did.

Then we clashed and the fight was on.

I found myself engaged with a blue warrior who wore around his waist a girdle of grisly spoils from the earlier encounter—severed human hands.

I decided to claim some recompense for those hands.

Being mounted, I was more at an advantage than I had been, for the Argzoon were not. Apart from the advance guard I had originally seen, there seemed to be few mounts among them and I concluded that their need for secrecy had made them wary of using too many.

The warrior struck at me left-handed, catching me by surprise. The weapon was a battle-axe, and it took all my skill to block the blow and at the same time avoid the lunge of his sword.

He pressed down on my sword with both weapons and we remained in that position for several moments, testing each other's strength and reflexes. Then he tried to raise the sword to aim a blow at my head, but I whipped my own blade out from under his axe and he was unbalanced for a second. I used that second to pierce him in the throat.

Meanwhile there was general confusion around me. Though it seemed we were beating the Argzoon, we had many casualties. It seemed we had only about half our original strength left.

I saw Darnad having trouble with a couple of blue warriors and rode in to help him.

Together we quickly despatched our opponents.

From the fifty Argzoon we had fought, only two had surrendered.

We used the same technique on them as we had used with the previous prisoners. At last they began to answer our questions surlily.

"Did you see any of your comrades take a Karnala woman with them?"

"Perhaps."

Darnad fingered his knife.

"Yes," said the Argzoon.

"In which direction were they riding?" I said.

"North."

"But where did you think they were going?"

"Maybe towards Narlet."

"Where is that?" I asked Darnad.

"About three days' ride—a brigand town near the borders of the Crimson Plain."

"A brigand town—dangerous for us, eh?"

"It could be," Darnad admitted. "But I doubt it if *we* don't make trouble. They prefer not to antagonize us if we make it plain we are not seeking any of their number. In fact," Darnad laughed, "I have a friend or two in Narlet. Rogues, but pleasant company if you forget that they are thieves and murderers many times over."

Again we put the prisoners in the charge of one man and our somewhat depleted force moved on towards Narlet.

At least we had some definite information and our spirits rose as we rode full speed towards the City of Thieves.

Twice more *en route* we were forced to stop and engage Argzoon and the prisoners we took confirmed that in all likelihood Shizala had been taken to Narlet.

Less than three days later we saw a range of hills in the far distance, marking the end of the Crimson Plain.

Then we saw a small walled city—its wall seeming to be built of logs covered with dried mud.

The buildings were square and seemed solid enough, but they had little beauty.

We had reached Narlet, City of Thieves.

But would we find Shizala?

CHAPTER EIGHT

THE CITY OF THIEVES

IT would not be true to say that we received a joyous welcome in Narlet but, as Darnad had said, they did not immediately set upon us, though they gave us looks of intense suspicion and tended to avoid us as we entered the city's only gate and made our way through the narrow streets.

"We'll get no information from most of them," Darnad told me. "But I think I know where I can find someone who will help us—if Old Belet Vor still lives."

"Belet Vor?" I said questioningly.

"One of those friends I mentioned."

Our little party emerged into a market square of some sort and Darnad pointed to a small house sandwiched between two ramshackle buildings. When I used to patrol these parts he saved my life once. I had the good fortune to return the favor—and somehow we struck up a strong friendship. One of those things."

We dismounted outside the house and from it an old man emerged. He was toothless and wrinkled and incredibly ugly, yet there was a jaunty appearance about him which made one forget his unwholesome visage.

"Ah, the Bradhinak Darnad—an honor, an honor." His eyes twinkled, belying his servile words. He spoke ironically. I could see why Darnad had liked him.

"Greetings, you old scoundrel. How many children have you robbed today?"

"Only a dozen or so, Bradhinak. Would this friend of yours like to see my spoils—some of the sweetmeats are only half-eaten. Heh—heh!"

"Spare us the temptation." I smiled as he ushered us into his hovel.

It was surprisingly clean and orderly and we sat on benches while he brought us basu.

Drinking the sweet beverage, Darnad said seriously: "We are in haste, Belet Vor. Have any warriors of the Argzoon been seen in Narlet recently—coming here perhaps a day or so before us?"

The old rogue cocked his head to one side. "Why, yes—two Argzoon warriors. Looked as if they'd taken a beating and were scampering back to their mountain lairs."

"Just two warriors?"

Belet Vor chuckled. "And two prisoners, by the look of them. I'm thinking they wouldn't have chosen such company of their own free will."

"*Two* prisoners?"

"Women, both of them. One fair, one dark."

"Shizala and Horguhl!" I cried.

"Are they still here?" Darnad asked urgently.

"I'm not sure. They could have left early this morning, but I think not."

"Where are they staying?"

"Ah—there you have it, if you seek the prisoners. The Argzoon warriors seem to be of high rank. They are guests of our city's noble Bradhi."

"Your Bradhi—not Chinod Sai?"

"Yes. He has now chosen to call himself the Bradhi Chinod Sai. Narlet is becoming respectable, eh? He is one of your peers now, Bradhinak Darnad—not so?"

"The scoundrel. He gives himself airs."

"Perhaps," said old Belet Vor musingly, "but I seem to remember that many of the established nations in these parts had origins similar to ours."

Darnad laughed shortly. "You have me there, Belet Vor—but that's for posterity. I know Chinod Sai for a blood-thirsty slayer of women and children."

"You do him an injustice." Belet Vor grinned. "He has killed at least one youth in a fair fight."

Darnad turned to me, speaking seriously. "If these Argzoon have Chinod Sai's protection, then we will have greater difficulty getting Shizala—and this other woman—out of their power. We are in a bad position."

"I have a suggestion, if you will hear it," Belet Vor insinuated.

"I'll listen to anything reasonable," said Darnad.

"Well—I would say that the Argzoon and their ladies are guesting in the special chambers set aside for sudden visitors of some standing."

"What of it?" I said, a trifle tersely.

"Those chambers are conveniently placed on the ground floor. They have large windows. Perhaps you could help your friends without—er—actually disturbing our royal Bradhi?"

I frowned. "But aren't they guarded?"

"Oh, there are guards surrounding the great Bradhi's palace at intervals. He fears, possibly, that there may be robbers in these parts—such little faith does he have in his subjects."

"How would we enter the guest rooms without the guards seeing us?" I rubbed my chin.

"You would have to dispose of them—they are very alert. After all, some of the best thieves of the Crimson Plain have tried to help themselves to Chinod Sai's booty from time to time. A few have even succeeded. Most have helped decorate the city walls—or at least their heads have."

"But how could we silence the guards easily?"

"That," said Belet Vor with a wink, "is where I can help you. Excuse me." He got up and hobbled from the room.

"I think he's a likeable old bandit, don't you?" Darnad said when Belet Vor had left.

I nodded. "But he puts himself in danger, surely, by helping us. If we are successful this Chinod Sai's men are bound to suspect that he had a hand in it."

"True. But I doubt whether Chinod Sai would do anything about it. Belet Vor knows many secrets and some of them concern Chinod Sai. Also, Belet Vor is very popular and Chinod Sai sits on his self-made throne rather uncertainly. There are many who would usurp him if they could gain a popular following. If anything happened to Belet Vor it would be just the excuse needed by some would-be Bradhi of Thieves. Chinod Sai knows that well enough."

"Good," I replied. "But nonetheless, I think he risks more than he needs for our sake."

"I told you, Michael Kane—there is a bond between us."

That simple statement meant a great deal to Darnad, evidently, and I think I knew how he felt. Such virtues as loyalty, self-discipline, temperance, moderation, truthfulness, fortitude and honŏrable conduct to women are apparently outmoded in the societies of New York, London and Paris—but on Mars, my Vashu, they were still strong. Is it any wonder I should prefer the Red Planet to my own?

Soon Belet Vor returned carrying a long tube and a small, handsomely worked box.

"These will silence your guards," he said, flourishing the box. "And more—they will not actually kill them."

He opened the box carefully and displayed the contents. About a score of tiny, feathered slivers lay there. At once I guessed that the tube was a blow-pipe and these were its ammunition. The slivers must be tipped with some poison that would knock the guards out.

In silence we accepted the weapon.

"There are some eight shatis until nightfall," Belet Vor said. "Time to exchange reminiscences, eh? How many men came with you?"

"There are six left," I said.

"Then there is room enough in here for them. Invite them in for a cup of basu."

Darnad went outside to extend Belet Vor's invitation to his men.

They came in and accepted the cups gratefully. Belet Vor also brought food.

The eight shatis passed with incredible slowness and I spent them, for the most part, in thoughtful silence. Soon, if providence were on our side, I would see Shizala again! My heart pounded in spite of myself. I knew she could never be mine—but just to be

near her would be enough, to know that she was safe,
to know that I would always be nearby to protect her.

When it was dark Belet Vor glanced at me.

"Eight is a good number," he said. "Not too small
a force if you run into trouble, not so large as to be
easily detected."

We rose, our war-harness creaking, our accoutre-
ments jingling. We rose in silence save for those small
sounds.

"Farewell, Darnad," Belet Vor grasped the young
Bradhinak's shoulder and Darnad grasped the old
man's. There seemed to be something final about that
parting, as if Belet Vor knew they would never meet
again.

"Farewell, Belet Vor," he said softly. Their eyes
met for an instant and then Darnad was striding for
the door.

"Thank you, Belet Vor," I said.

"Good luck," he murmured as we left and followed
Darnad towards Chinod Sai's 'palace'.

The building we finally came upon was situated in
the centre of the city. It was only two stories high and
while it had some stone in its construction it was
mainly of wood.

It stood in an open square from which several narrow streets radiated. We hugged the shadows of the
streets and watched the guards as they patrolled the
grounds of the palace.

Belet Vor had told Darnad exactly where the guest
rooms were and when the Argzoon were likely to retire. We assumed that Shizala and Horguhl would not
be dining with Chinod Sai. At this time it was likely
that the Argzoon were eating in the main hall of the
building. This meant we might be able to rescue the

two women without arousing the suspicion of those inside and thus avoid a noisy fight.

After we had ascertained the exact movements of the patrolling guards, Darnad placed the first dart carefully in the blow-pipe and took aim.

His aim was accurate. The dart winged its way towards the guard. I saw him clutch his neck and then fall almost soundlessly to the ground.

The next guard—there were four we needed to attend to in all—saw his comrade fall and rushed towards him. We heard him lean over him and speak casually. "Get up, Akar, or the Bradhi will have your head. I told you not to drink so much before we went on guard!"

I held my breath as Darnad aimed another dart, expelled it softly—and the second guard fell.

The third guard turned a corner and paused in astonishment on seeing the bodies of his fallen comrades.

"Hey! What's this—?"

He would never fully know, for Darnad's third dart took him in his naked shoulder. The drug was quick. The guard fell. Darnad grinned at me—we seemed near to success.

The fourth guard was disposed of even before he saw his fellows.

Then the eight of us moved in, cat-footing it towards the guest rooms.

Soon, soon, I thought, all this would be over and we could return to Varnal to live in peace. I could study the sciences of the mysterious Sheev, increase the inventions that the Karnala would be able to use. With my help, the Karnala need never fear attack again. They had the basic technology necessary for building internal combustion engines, electric power generators, radios—I could accomplish all that for them.

Those were the thoughts—inapt, perhaps, for the moment—that coursed through my brain as we crept towards the guest room windows.

The windows were not glazed, only shuttered, and one of these was drawn back. Luck seemed to be on our side that night.

Cautiously I peered into the room. It was richly furnished, though somewhat vulgarly, floors heaped with furs, carved chests and benches. In a bracket a torch flared, illuminating the room. It was empty.

I swung my leg over the low sill and entered the room as quietly as I could.

Darnad and the others followed me.

Then we all stood there, staring at one another, listening intently for some sound that might indicate where the women were imprisoned.

It came at last—a low tone that could have been anything. All we could be sure of was that it issued from a human throat.

It came from a room on our left.

Darnad and I went towards the room, with the warriors following. We paused at the door which, surprisingly, was unbarred.

Now from within came a sound that seemed like a soft laugh—a woman's laugh. But it could not be a laugh. I must have misheard. The next sound was a voice, pitched low and impossible to make sense of.

Darnad looked at me. Our eyes met, and then with a concerted movement we flung open the door.

Torchlight showed us the two within.

One was Horguhl, standing close to the window.

The other was Shizala—my Shizala!

Shizala was bound hand and foot.

But Horguhl was unfettered. She stood with hands on hips smiling down at Shizala, who glared back at her.

Horguhl's smile froze when she saw us. Shizala gave a glad cry: "Michael Kane! Darnad! Oh, thank Zar you have come!"

Horguhl stood there expressionlessly, saying nothing.

I stepped forward to untie Shizala. As I worked at her bonds I kept a suspicious eye on the Vladnyar girl, uncertain of her part in this. Was she or was she not a prisoner?

It did not seem likely now. Yet . . .

Horguhl suddenly laughed in my face.

I finished untying Shizala's bonds. "Why do you laugh?" I asked.

"I thought you were dead," she replied, not answering my question. And then she lifted her head and let out a piercing shriek.

"Silence!" Darnad said in a fierce whisper. "You will alert the whole palace. We intend you no harm."

"I am sure you do not," she said as Darnad stepped towards her. "But I mean *you* harm my friends!" Again she shrieked.

There was a disturbance outside in the corridor.

Shizala's eyes glistened with tears—but with gladness also—as she stared up into my face. "Oh, Michael Kane—somehow I knew you would save me. I thought they had killed you—and yet . . ."

"No time for conversation," I said brusquely, trying to hide the emotion that her closeness brought to my breast. "We must escape."

Darnad had his hand over Horguhl's mouth. He looked unhappy, not used to treating a woman so.

"Horguhl is no prisoner," Shizala said. "She—"

"I can see that now," I said. "Come—we must hurry."

We turned and left the room. Darnad released his hold on Horguhl and followed us.

But before we could reach the window a score of men, led by the two Argzoon giants and another who wore a bright circlet on his matted, greasy hair, burst into the room.

Darnad, myself and our six warriors turned to face them, forming a barrier between them and Shizala.

"Leave quickly, Shizala," I said softly. "Go to the house of Belet Vor." I gave her brief instructions how to find the old man.

"I cannot leave you. I cannot."

"You must—it will serve us better if we know you, at least, are safe. Please do as I say." I was staring at the Argzoon and the others, waiting for them to attack. They were moving in cautiously.

She seemed to understand my reasoning and it was with relief that I saw her from the corner of my eye clamber over the sill and disappear into the night.

Horguhl emerged from the other room, pointing an imperious finger at us. Her face was flushed with anger.

"These men sought to abduct me and the other woman," she said to the greasy-haired man who stood there with drawn sword.

"So—did you not know," he said, addressing us with a leer, "that Chinod Sai values the safety of his guests and resents the intrusion of riff-raff such as you?"

"Riff-raff, murderer of children," said Darnad. "I know you upstart—you who calls himself Bradhi of a collection of cut-throats and pilferers!"

Chinod Sai sneered. "You speak bravely—but your words are hollow. You are all about to die."

Then he and his unholy allies were on us, his guards supporting them.

The duel began.

I found myself fighting not only Chinod Sai but one of the Argzoon, and it was all I could do to defend myself, even though I knew I outmatched them both in swordsmanship.

However, they tended to crowd each other and this, at least, was to my advantage.

I held them off as best I could until I saw my chance. Rapidly I flung my sword from my right hand to my left. This foxed them for a second. Then I lunged at the Argzoon, who was slower than Chinod Sai, and caught him in the breast. He fell back groaning. That left the self-styled Bradhi of Narlet.

But seeing the great blue warrior fall, Chinod Sai evidently lost his stomach for battle and backed away, letting his hired guards take his place.

It was my turn to sneer.

One by one our own warriors went down until only Darnad and myself were left standing.

I hardly cared if I died. So long as Shizala were safe—and I knew that the wily old Belet Vor would see to that—I was prepared to die.

But I did not die. There were so many warriors pressing in towards us that we could hardly move our sword arms.

Soon we were not so much sword-fighting as wrestling.

Their weight of numbers was too great. After a short time we were engulfed and, for the second time in the space of a week, I received a blow on the head— and this second blow was not meant in kindness as the first had been!

My senses fled, blackness engulfed me, and I knew no more.

CHAPTER NINE

BURIED ALIVE!

I opened my eyes but saw nothing. I smelt much. My nostrils were assailed by a foul, damp, chilly smell that seemed to indicate I was somewhere below ground. I flexed my arms and legs. They were unbound, at least.

I tried to get up but bumped my head. I could only crouch on the damp, messy ground.

I was horrified. Had I been incarcerated in some tomb? Was I to die slowly of hunger, or have my senses leave me? With an effort I controlled myself. Then I heard a slight sound to my left.

Cautiously I felt about me and my hand touched something warm.

Someone groaned. I had touched a limb. It stirred.

Then a voice murmured: "Who is there? Where am I?"

"Darnad?"

"Yes."

"It is Michael Kane. We seem to be in some sort of dungeon—with a very low ceiling indeed."

"What?" I heard Darnad move and sit up, perhaps reaching with his hands above him. "No!"

111

"Do you know the place?"

"I believe I have heard of it."

"What is it?"

"The old heating system."

"That sounds very innocuous. What's that?"

"Narlet is built on the ancient ruins of one of the Sheev cities. Hardly anything of it exists, save the foundations of one particular building. Those foundations now make up Chinod Sai's foundations for his palace. Apparently the slabs forming the floor of the palace lie over an ancient, sunken pool which could be filled with hot water and made to heat the ground floor of the palace—perhaps the whole of it—by means of pipes. From what I hear, the Sheev abandoned this particular city well before their decline, for they later discovered better methods of heating."

"And so we are buried under the floor of Chinod Sai's palace?"'"

"I've heard it gives him pleasure to imprison his enemies here—having them permanently at his feet, as it were."

I did not laugh, though I admired the fortitude of my friend in jesting at a time like this.

I put my hands up and felt the smooth, damp slabs over my head, pressing on them. They did not budge.

"If he can raise the slabs, why can't we?"

"There are only a few loose ones, I've heard—Belet Vor told me all this—and very heavy furniture is placed over those when prisoners have been incarcerated."

"So we *have* been buried alive," I said, suppressing a shudder of terror. I admit that I was horrified. I think any man—no matter how brave—would have been at the thought of such a fate.

"Yes." Darnad's voice was a thin mutter. It seemed that he, too, had no liking for what had happened to us.

"At least we have saved Shizala," I reminded him. "Belet Vor will see that she returns safely to Varnal."

"Yes." The voice sounded slightly less strained.

Silence for a while.

Later I made up my mind.

"If you will stay where you are, Darnad," I said, "so that I may keep some sort of bearing, I will explore our prison."

"Very well," he agreed.

I had to crawl, of course—there was no other way.

I counted the number of 'paces' as I moved across that horribly wet and foul-smelling floor.

By the time I had counted to sixty-one I had reached a wall. I then began to crawl round this, still counting.

Something obstructed me. I could not tell at first what it was. Thin objects like sticks. I felt them carefully and then withdrew my hand suddenly as I realized what they were. Bones. One of Chinod Sai's earlier victims.

I encountered several more skeletons on my circuit of the walls.

From where I had started, the first wall measured ninety-seven 'paces'; the second only fifty-four. The third was, in all, a hundred and twenty-six. I began to wonder why I was doing this, save to keep my mind occupied.

The fourth wall. One 'pace', two, three . . .

On the seventeenth 'pace' along the fourth wall my hand touched—nothing!

Surely this could not be a means of escape? By

touch I discovered that some sort of circular hole led
off from the fourth wall—perhaps a pipe that had
once brought water into the chamber. It was just wide
enough to take a man.

I put my head inside and reached my arms along
it. It was wet and slimy but nothing stopped me.

Before I raised Darnad's hopes, I decided to see
whether the pipe really offered a chance of escape.

I squeezed my whole body into it and began to lever
myself forward, wriggling like a snake.

I began to feel elated when nothing obstructed me.
Soon my whole body was in the pipe. I wriggled on.
I hate being so confined normally, but if the pipe
meant escape it was worth suffering my claustropho-
bia.

But then came disappointment.

My questing hands found something—and I knew
at once what they touched.

It was another human skeleton.

Evidently some other poor soul—perhaps many—
had sought this means of escape and had been disap-
pointed—and not had the energy or inclination to return.

I sighed deeply and began to wriggle back down.

But as I did so I suddenly heard something from
behind me. I paused. It was the sound of grating
stone. A little light filtered up the pipe and I heard
someone chuckle.

I did not move. I waited.

Then came Chinod Sai's jeering voice. "Greetings,
Bradhinak—how are you enjoying your stay?"

Darnad did not reply.

"Come up, come up—I wish to show my men what
a real Bradhinak of the Karnala looks like. A little

befouled, perhaps—I am sorry my accommodation is
not quite what you are accustomed to."

"I'd rather stay here than be subjected to your insults, you scum," Darnad replied levelly.

"And what of your friend—the strange one? Perhaps he would like a little respite. Where is he?"

"I do not know."

"You do not know! But he was put down there with
you. Do not lie, boy—where is your companion?"

"I do not know."

The light increased, probably because Chinod Sai
was peering into his horrible crypt, using a torch for
illumination.

His voice rose querulously. "He *must* be down
there!"

Darnad's tone seemed lighter now. "You can see
he is not—unless one of these skeletons is his."

"Impossible! Guards!"

I heard the faint sound of feet above me.

Chinod Sai continued: "Take up some more of
these stones—see if the other prisoner is hiding in a
corner. He is down here somewhere. Meanwhile,
bring up the Karnala."

More sounds, and I gathered that Darnad had been
escorted away.

Then I heard the guards beginning to tear up other
slabs and I grinned to myself, hoping that they would
not think of looking in the pipe. Then something occurred to me. It was not a pleasant thought but it
might save me and give me, in turn, a chance to save
Darnad.

I wriggled up the pipe again and reached up to take
hold of some of the bones of the unfortunate who had
been there before me. He had not been lucky but, even

though dead some years, he might be able to help me now—and help me avenge him if and when the opportunity came.

Squeezing myself up against one section of the pipe as tightly as I could, I began to pass bones down in front of me until quite a heap lay below my feet. I did this as soundlessly as possible, and any noise I did make was probably drowned by the racket the desperate guards were making pulling up flagstones and crawling around in the semidarkness trying to find me.

"He isn't here," I heard one of them say.

"You are a fool," answered another. "He must be here!"

"Well, I tell you he isn't. Come and look for yourself."

Another guard joined the first and I heard him stumbling around, too.

"I don't understand—there is no way out of here. We've put enough of them down here one time or another. Hey—what's this?"

The guard had found the pipe. The light increased.

"Could he have gone up here? If he did it won't do him any good. It's blocked at the other end!"

Then the guard found the bones. "Ugh! He didn't go up, but someone else tried to. These bones are old."

"What are we going to tell the Bradhi?" The first guard spoke nervously. "This smacks of magic!"

"There's no such thing!"

"So we're told these days, but my grandfather says there are stories . . ."

"Shut your mouth! Magic—ghosts. Nonsense . . . Still, I must admit that he had a strange look about him. He seemed to belong to no nation I've ever seen.

And I have heard that beyond the ocean lies another
land where men have powers greater than normal.
And then there are the Sheev . . ."

"The Sheev! That's it!"

"Hold your tongue. Chinod Sai will tear it out if
he hears such language spoken in his palace!"

"What do we tell him?"

"Only the facts. The man *was* here—but he is no
longer here."

"But will he believe us?"

"We must hope that he does."

I heard the guards clamber up and march away.
The instant they had gone I slipped down the pipe as
fast as I could and was soon standing up in what had
been my prison, my head just above the level of the
floor. Flagstones had been ripped out and the whole
floor was in a mess. I was glad of that, at least.

No one was in the room, which seemed to be some
sort of throne room judging by the huge, ornately
carved, precious-metal gilded chair at one end.

I heaved myself up and stood in the room. As
swiftly and as silently as I could, I ran towards the
door and stood by it, listening.

It was half open. Angry voices came from the other
side.

There were more sounds coming from outside the
palace itself—shouts, cries. They sounded angry.

Somewhere in the distance several pairs of fists
began to beat on a door.

Then I stepped back as, suddenly, someone came
into the room.

It was Chinod Sai.

He stared at me in horror for a moment.

That moment was all I needed. In a flash I had

darted forward and snatched his own sword from his belt!

I pressed the point gently against his throat and said with a grim smile on my lips: "Call for your guards, Chinod Sai—and you call for death!"

He paled and gurgled something. I gestured for him to come into the room and shut the door. I had been lucky. Everyone had been too busy with whatever else they were concerned with to notice what had happened to their 'Bradhi'.

"Speak in a low voice," I ordered. "Tell me what is happening and where my comrade is."

"How—how did you escape?"

"I am asking the questions, my friend. Now—answer!"

He grunted. "What do you mean?"

"Answer!"

"The scum are attacking my palace," he said. "Some petty dahara-thief seeks to replace me."

"I hope he makes a better chief than you. And where is my comrade?"

He waved a hand behind him.

"In there."

Suddenly someone entered. I had expected the guards to knock and had intended that Chinod Sai should tell them not to enter.

But this was not a guard.

It was the surviving Argzoon. He looked astonished to see me. He turned, giving a roar of warning to the men in the room.

They came in and I backed away, looking around for a means of escape, but all the windows in this room were barred.

"Kill him!" screamed Chinod Sai, pointing a shaking finger at me. "Kill him!"

Led by the blue Argzoon, the guards came at me. I knew that I faced death—they would not take me a prisoner a second time.

CHAPTER TEN

INTO THE CAVES OF DARKNESS

SOMEHOW I managed to keep them at bay, though I will never know how. Then I saw Darnad appear behind them, waving a sword he had got from somewhere.

Together, one on each side, we took on Chinod Sai and his men, but we knew we must be beaten eventually.

Then there came a sudden, elated roar, and bursting into the throne room came a wild mob waving swords, spears and halberds.

They were led by a good-looking young man, and by the gleam in his eyes—at once calculating and triumphant—I guessed him to be the next contender for the paltry throne of the City of Thieves.

Now, while the others helped Darnad deal with the Argzoon and the guards, I concentrated on Chinod Sai. This time, I promised myself, he would not retreat.

Chinod Sai realized my intention and this seemed to improve his skill.

Back and forth across the broken floor of the throne

room, over the bones of the wretches he had incarcerated for his own perverted pleasure, we fought.

Lunging, parrying, thrusting, the steel of our blades rang through the hall while to one side the mob fought, a thick mass of struggling men.

Then came disaster for me—or so I thought. I tripped over one of the flagstones and fell backwards into the pit!

I saw Chinod Sai raise his arm for the thrust that would finish me as, sprawled out on the slime, I stared up at him.

Then, as the sword came towards my heart I rolled away, under part of the floor that was still intact. I heard him curse and saw him drop down after me. He saw me and lunged. Raising myself on my left arm, I returned his lunge and caught him exactly in the heart. I pushed home my thrust and he fell back with a groan.

I climbed from the pit. "A fitting burial place, Chinod Sai," I said. "Lie with the bones of those you have slain so horribly. You had a swifter death than you deserved!"

I was just in time to see Darnad dispose of the last Argzoon.

The fight was over and the young leader of the mob raised his right hand high, shouting:

"Chinod Sai is defeated—the tyrant dies!"

The mob replied exultantly: "Salute Morda Kohn, Bradhi of Narlet!"

Morda Kohn swung round and grinned at me. "Enemies of Chinod Sai are friends of mine. Indirectly you helped me gain the throne. But where is Chinod Sai?"

I pointed at the floor. "I slew him," I said simply.

Morda Kohn laughed. "Good, good! You are even more of a friend for that little service."

"It was no service to you," I said, "but something I had promised myself the pleasure of accomplishing."

"Quite so. I was truly sorry about the death of your friend."

"My friend?" I said as Darnad joined us. He had a flesh wound on his right shoulder but otherwise seemed all right.

"Belet Vor—did you not know?"

"What has happened to Belet Vor?" Darnad asked urgently.

I must admit I was not only thinking of Belet Vor—but of the girl I had sent to him, Shizala.

"Why, that is what enabled me to arouse the people against Chinod Sai," Morda Kohn said. "Chinod Sai and his blue friend learned that you had been seen in the house of Belet Vor. They went there and they ordered him to be beheaded on the spot!"

"Belet Vor, dead? Beheaded—oh, no!" Darnad's face turned pale with horror.

"I am afraid so."

"But the girl we rescued—the one we sent to him?" I spoke in some trepidation, almost afraid to hear the answer.

"Girl? I do not know—I heard nothing of a girl. Perhaps she is still at his house, hiding somewhere."

I relaxed. That was probably true.

"There is still another missing," Darnad said. "The Vladnyar woman—Horguhl. Where is she?"

Together we searched the palace but there was no sign of her.

Night was falling as we borrowed mounts from the new 'Bradhi' and rushed to Belet Vor's house.

Inside, it had been torn apart. We called Shizala's name but she did not answer.

Shizala had gone—but where? And how?

We stumbled out of the house. Had we fought and risked so much only to fail now?

Back to the palace to see if Morda Kohn could help us.

The new Bradhi was supervising the replacement of the flagstones. "They will be securely cemented down," he said. "They will never be put to the same dreadful use again."

"Morda Kohn," I said desperately, "the girl was not at Belet Vor's house. And we know she would not have gone anywhere of her own accord. Did any of Chinod Sai's guards survive? If they did, one of them may be able to tell us what happened."

"I think there are several prisoners in the ante-room." Morda Kohn nodded. "Question them if you like."

We went to the ante-room. There were three sulking, badly wounded prisoners.

"Do any of you know where Shizala is?" I asked.

"Shizala?" One of them looked up with a frown.

"The blonde girl—the prisoner who was here."

"Oh, her—I think they both went off together."

"Both?"

"Her and the dark-haired woman."

"Where did they go?"

"What's it worth to tell you what I know?" The guard looked cunningly at me.

"I will speak to Morda Kohn. He owes us a favor. I will ask him to show mercy to you."

"You'll keep your word?"

"Of course."

"I think they went to the Mountains of Argzoon."

"Ah—but why?" Darnad broke in. "Why should a Vladnyar willingly go to Argzoon? The Blue Giants are no-one's friends."

"There is something mysterious about Horguhl's association with the Argzoon. Perhaps when we find her we will learn the answer," I said. "Could you lead us to the Mountains of Argzoon, Darnad?"

"I think so." He nodded.

"Come, then—let's make haste after them. With luck we may even catch them before they reach the mountains."

"Best that we did," he said.

"Why?"

"Because the Argzoon literally dwell in the mountains—in the Caves of Darkness that run *under* the range. Some say it is really the Bleak World of the Dead, and from what I've heard it's possible!"

We spoke briefly to Morda Kohn, telling him to show the guard mercy. Then we strode outside, mounted our daharas and rode into the night—heading for the dreadful Caves of Darkness.

We were not lucky. First Darnad's beast cut its foot on a sharp rock and went lame. We had to travel at walking pace for a full day until we came to a camp where we could exchange Darnad's prime mount for a rather stringy beast that looked as if it had little stamina.

Then we lost our bearings on a barren plain known as the Wilderness of Sorrow—and we could understand why anyone would feel sorrowful on encountering it.

On the other hand, the mount that Darnad had exchanged was in fact very strong—and my own beast wearied before his did!

We finally crossed the Wilderness of Sorrow and emerged on the shores of an incredibly wide river—wider even than the Mississippi.

Another pause while we borrowed a boat from a friendly fisherman and managed to cross. Luckily Darnad had a precious ring on his finger and was able to convert this into pearls, which were the general currency of these parts.

We bought supplies in the riverside town and learned—to our relief, for there had always been the chance that the guard was lying maliciously—that two women answering to the description of Horguhl and Shizala had passed that way. We enquired if Shizala had seemed to be under restraint, but our informant told us that she did not appear to be bound.

This was puzzling and we could not understand why Shizala should seem to be travelling to the terrible domain of the Argzoon of her own free will.

But, as we told ourselves, all this would be learned the quicker if we caught up with them. They were still some three days ahead of us.

So we crossed the Carzax River in the fisherman's boat, ferrying our mounts and provisions with us. It was a difficult task and the current drew us many miles down river before we reached the other side. The fisherman would collect the boat later. We pulled it ashore, strapped our provisions to our animals and mounted.

It was forest land now, but the trees were the strangest I had ever seen.

Their trunks were not solid like the tree-trunks on

Earth, but consisted of many hundreds of slender
stems curling around one another to form trunks
some thirty or forty feet in diameter. On the other
hand, the trees did not reach very high, but fanned
out so that sometimes when passing through a particular grove of low-growing trees our heads actually
stood out above the trees. It made me feel gigantic!

Also, the foliage had a tinge similar to the ferns of
the Crimson Plain—though red was only the main
color. There were also tints of blue, green and yellow,
brown and orange. It seemed, in fact, that the forest
was in a perpetual state of autumn and I was pleased
by the sight of it. Strange as the stumpy trees were
they reminded me, in some obscure way, of my boy-
hood.

Had it not been for the object of our quest, I would
have liked to relax more and spend longer in that
strange forest.

But there was something else in the forest that I was
to meet shortly—and that decided me, if nothing else
could have done, on the necessity of moving on.

We had been travelling in the forest for two days
when Darnad suddenly pulled his mount up short and
pointed silently through the foliage.

I could see nothing and shook my head in puzzle-
ment.

Darnad's beast now seemed to move a little rest-
lessly, and so did mine.

Darnad began to turn his dahara, pointing back the
way we had come. The peculiar, ape-like beast obeyed
the guiding reins and my own followed suit, rather
quickly, as if glad to be turning back.

Then Darnad stopped again and his hand fell to his
sword.

"Too late," he said. "And I should have warned you."

"I see nothing—I hear nothing. What should you have warned me of?"

"The *heela.*"

"Heela—what is a heela?"

"That—" Darnad pointed.

Skulking towards us, its hide exactly the same mottled shades as the foliage of the trees, came a beast out of a nightmare.

It had eight legs and each leg terminated in six curved talons. It had two heads and each head had a broad, gaping mouth full of long, razor-like teeth, glaring yellow eyes, flaring nostrils. A single neck rose from the trunk and then divided near the top to accommodate the heads.

It had two tails, scaly and powerful-looking, and a barrel-shaped body rippling with muscle.

It was unlike anything I could describe. It could not exist—but it did!

The heela stopped a few yards away and its twin tails lashed as it regarded us with its two pairs of eyes.

The only thing to its advantage, as far as I could see, was that it measured only about half the size of an ordinary dahara.

Yet it still looked dangerous and could easily dispose of me, I knew.

Then it sprang. Not at me and not at Darnad—but at the head of Darnad's dahara.

The poor animal shrieked in pain and fear as the heela sank its eight sets of talons into its great flat head and simply clung there, biting with its two sets of teeth at the dahara's spinal cord.

Darnad began to hack at the heela with his sword.

I tried to move in to help him but my animal refused to budge.

I dismounted—it was the only thing I could do—and paused behind the clinging heela's back. I did not know much about Martian biology, but I selected a spot on the heela's neck corresponding to the place where he was biting the dahara. I knew that many animals will go for a spot on other species which corresponds with their *own* vital spots.

I plunged my sword in.

For a few moments the heela still clung to the dahara's head; then it released its grip and with a blood-curdling scream of anguish and fury fell to the mossy ground. I stood back, ready to meet any attack it might make. But it got up, stood shakily on its legs, took a couple of paces away from me—and then fell dead.

Meanwhile, Darnad had dismounted from the dahara, now moaning in pain and stamping on the moss.

The poor beast's flesh had been ripped away from a considerable area of its head and neck. It was beyond any help we could give it—save to put it out of its pain.

Regretfully, I saw Darnad place his sword against the creature's head and drive it home, wincing as he did so.

Soon dahara and heela lay side by side. A useless waste of life, I reflected.

What was more, we should now have to ride double and though my dahara was stong enough to carry both of us, we should have to travel at about half our previous speed.

Bad luck was dogging us, it seemed.

Riding double, we left the heela-infested forest be-

hind. Darnad informed me that we had been lucky
to meet only one of the beasts since there had been
others of its pack about. Apparently it was quite common amongst heelas for the leader to attack the victim
first and, if successful, lead the rest in for the kill, having tested the victim's strength. If, on the other hand,
the heela-leader were killed, then the pack would
skulk off, judging the enemy too strong to risk attacking. Besides which they would feed off their dead leader's corpse. In this case, the corpse of the dahara, too.

It seemed that, like hyaena, the heelas were strong
but cowardly. I thanked providence for this trait, at
any rate!

Now the air grew colder—we had been travelling
for well over a month—and the skies darker. We
began to cross a vast plain of black mud and obsidian
rock, stunted, sinister shrubs and ancient ruins. The
feet of our single dahara splashed in deep puddles or
waded through oozing mud, slipped on the glassy
rock or stumbled over great areas of broken masonry.

I asked Darnad if these were the ruins of the Sheev
but he muttered that he did not think so.

"I suspect that these ruins were once inhabited by
the Yaksha," he said.

I shivered as cold rain fell on us.

"Who were the Yaksha?"

"It is said they are ancient enemies of the Sheev but
originally of the same race."

"That is all you know?"

"Those are the only facts. The rest is superstition
and speculation." He seemed to shudder inwardly,
not from the cold but from some idea that had occurred to him.

On we went, making slower and slower progress

over that dark wasteland, taking shelter at night—
scarcely distinguishable though it was from day!—
under half-fallen walls or outcrops of rock. Strange,
livid beasts prowled that plain; peculiar cries like the
voices of lost souls; queer disturbances that we *felt*
rather than heard or saw.

It was like that for another two weeks until the
looming crags of Argzoon became visible through the
dim, misty light of the Wastes of Doom.

The Mountains of Argzoon were tall and jagged,
black and forbidding.

"Seeing their environment," I said to Darnad, "I
can understand why the Argzoon are what they are,
for such landscapes are not conducive to instilling a
sense of sweetness and light into one."

"I agree," he replied. Then a little later: "We
should reach the Gates of Gor Delpus before nightfall."

"What are they?"

"The entrance to the Caves of Darkness. They are,
I've been told, never guarded, for few have ever dared
venture into the Argzoon's own underground land—
they let our normal fear of dark, enclosed spaces do
their work for them."

"Are the Caves very dangerous?"

"I do not know," he said. "No one has ever returned to tell . . ."

By nightfall we made out the Gates by means of
Deimos's very dim moonlight. They were mainly natural cave-mouths widened and made taller by crude
workmanship. They were dark and gloomy and I
could understand what Darnad had told me.

Only my mission—to rescue the woman I loved but

would never be able to make mine—would induce me to enter.

We left our faithful dahara outside to fend for himself until we returned—if ever we should.

And then we entered the Caves of Darkness.

CHAPTER ELEVEN

QUEEN OF THE ARGZOON

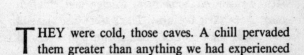

T HEY were cold, those caves. A chill pervaded
them greater than anything we had experienced
on the Wastes of Doom.

Down and down we went, along a smooth, broad,
winding track that had torches lighting it at wide intervals. We caught glimpses of vast grottos and caverns, as it were within the great caverns; of stalactites
and stalagmites; of jumbled, black rock and rivulets
of ice-cold water; of a bitter-smelling slime that clung
to the rocks; of small, pallid animals that scuttled
away at our approach.

And deeper down the sides of the path had been
decorated with trophies of war—here a skeleton of an
Argzoon in full armor, with sword, shield, spear and
axe, grinning down at us from its great height; there
several human skulls piled into a rough pyramid.
Dark trophies, brought alive sometimes by the flickering torchlight, but fitting decoration for this strange
place.

Then at length we felt the path turn sharply to the
left. Following it round, we suddenly came upon a
monstrous cave, its walls so far away they were invisi-

133

ble. We stood above it, looking down. The path led
to it, we could see, twisting down for perhaps two
miles. Huge fires flared at intervals on the floor of the
cave and there were complete villages dotted across
it. Fairly close to our side of the cave there was a stone
city—a city that seemed piled on blocks of stone
heaped almost haphazardly one upon the other. A
heavy city, a cold, strong, bleak city. A city to suit
the Argzoon.

Moving about in the city and the surrounding villages, we saw Argzoon men, women and children
going about their business. There were also pens of
dahara and some sort of small creature that seemed
to be a domestic version of the heela.

"How can we get in there?" I whispered to Darnad.
"They will realize who we are immediately!"

Just then I heard a noise behind us and pulled him
into the shadows of the rock.

A few moments later a group of some thirty Argzoon warriors stumbled past. They looked as if they
had been through an ordeal. Many bore untreated
wounds, others had had their armor almost completely cut to shreds, and all were weary.

I realized that these were probably survivors of the
'mopping up' operation instituted from Varnal the
day we had left.

That was another reason why we should not expose
ourselves! The Argzoon would enjoy taking vengeance on members of the race that had defeated
them.

But these warriors were too tired even to notice us.
They just staggered on down the twisting path towards the cavern world, where the great bonfires

crackled and attempted to heat and light the place with little success.

We could not wait for nightfall here, for it was perpetual night! How *could* we reach the city and discover where Shizala was imprisoned?

There was nothing for it but to begin creeping down the path, keeping to the shadows as best we could, hoping that the Argzoon would be too busy with their own affairs, treating their wounded, assessing their strength and so on, to notice us.

Not once did either of us think of returning to find help. It seemed too late for that. We must rescue Shizala ourselves.

But then it occurred to me!

Who else knew where Shizala was held? Who else had all the information concerning the Argzoon that we had?

The answer was plain—none.

When we had gone a little distance I turned to Darnad and said bluntly:

"You must go back."

"Go back? Are you mad?"

"No—I'm perfectly sane for once. Don't you realize that if we are both killed in this attempt, then there can be no further attempts to save Shizala—for what we know will die with us!"

"I had not thought of that," he mused. "But why should I go back? You go. I will try to . . ."

"No. You know the geography of Vashu better than I. I might easily get lost. Now you have led me to the Mountains of Argzoon you must return to the nearest friendly settlement, send messengers to tell where I am, where Shizala is—get the news out as fast as you can. Then a big force of warriors can come here while the Argzoon are still depleted and recovering and wipe out the threat of the Blue Giants once and for all!"

"But it will take me weeks to get back to civilization of any sort. If you get into trouble here you will be dead long before I can bring help."

"If personal safety were our first consideration," I reminded him, "neither of us would be here now. You must see the logic of what I say. Go!"

He thought deeply for a moment, then clapped me on the shoulder, turned and began to make his way rapidly back in the direction we had come.

Once made up, Darnad's mind made him act swiftly.

Now I crept on, feeling somehow even smaller and weaker in the face of monstrous nature now that Darnad had gone.

Somehow I managed to get to the base of the path without being seen.

Somehow I managed to dash from cliff-wall to the shadow of the city and hug myself close to the rough-hewn stone.

And then, all of a sudden, it became darker!

I could not at first understand the cause of my good luck. Then I saw that they were damping down the big fires!

Why?

Then I realized what must be happening. Fuel itself must be scarce so, for a period corresponding to night-time on the surface, the fires were damped while the Argzoon slept. In the almost pitch-black darkness I decided that this was my chance to explore the city and try to find out where Shizala was imprisoned.

Perhaps, if luck continued to stay on my side, I

would even have a chance to rescue her, and together we could leave the gloomy cavern-world of the Argzoon and ride back to Varnal.

I hardly dared consider this as I began slowly to climb the rough sides of the city wall.

It was a stiff climb, but not too difficult. Both my hands and my feet had been hardened over the long weeks of our quest and so I found I could grip the rock like a Gibraltar monkey.

The darkness brought its own dangers, of course, and I was forced to climb largely by touch, but soon I was on top of the wall.

Crouching, sword in hand just in case I should be surprised, I sidled along the wall, peering down into the city, trying to make out the likeliest place where Shizala might be held.

Then I saw it!

One building was fairly well illuminated by torches from within and brands on the ramparts. But this is not what I noticed so much as the great, brooding banner that flew from a mast on the central keep of the building.

It was the N'aal Banner that adorned Horguhl's tent on the battlefield outside—a larger version, but the same design.

It was little to go on—but it was something. I would make for the building with the banner.

I resheathed my sword and clambered over the other side of the wall, beginning to climb slowly down towards the ground.

I was nearly at the bottom with perhaps only a dozen feet to go when a detachment of Argzoon warriors suddenly rounded a building near the wall and marched towards me. I wondered if I had been seen—

whether they had been sent to deal with me. But then they began to pass beneath me. I was only a couple of feet above the head of the tallest as he passed. I clung like a fly to the wall, praying that I would not slip and betray myself.

As soon as they were out of sight, I climbed the remaining distance to the ground and dashed across to the cover of a building, fashioned from the same roughly-heaped stone as the wall.

Knowing that the Argzoon warriors had not had many mounts, I guessed that only a few had returned as yet, which explained why the city seemed virtually deserted.

This was another thing that I welcomed and which was to my advantage.

Soon I had reached the building I was headed for.

The sides of this were somewhat smoother, but I thought I could tackle it. The only problem here was that the walls were fairly well illuminated and I might be seen.

There was nothing for it but to risk it, for no other time would be better. I would try to reach a window and swing myself in. Once inside the building I might be able to hide myself better and at least discover something, by watching and listening, of where Shizala was being kept.

I got a hold on a piece of projecting stone and hauled myself up, inch by inch. It was slow going and increasingly difficult. All the windows—little more than holes in the rock—were some distance above the ground, none less than twenty feet, and the one I had decided to try was probably higher. I deduced that fear of attack was the reason why the windows were positioned so high.

But at last I managed to make the window and peered over the sill to see if the room beyond was occupied. It did not appear to be.

I entered quickly.

It appeared that I was in a store-room of some kind, for there were wicker baskets of dried fruit and meat, herbs and vegetables. I decided to make use of some of the food stuff, obviously looted in an earlier raiding expedition. I selected the most palatable items and ate them. I was thirsty, too, but there was no readily available source of water. I would have to wait for a drink.

Feeling refreshed, I explored the room. It was fairly large and very draughty. Perhaps because of the draughts, it had not been used as a living accommodation for a long while—judging by the old and near-rotted pieces of basket that littered the floor.

I found the door and tried it.

To my great disappointment it was locked—barred from the outside, probably as a precaution against thieves!

I was very weary and my eyes kept closing involuntarily as I fought sleep. The pursuit had been long and arduous; we had allowed ourselves little time for rest. I decided that I would be more use to Shizala if I were rested.

I clambered over the baskets and made myself a kind of nest in the centre by removing some baskets and piling them around me. That way I would be warmer, and if anyone entered the room they would not see me. Feeling fairly secure, I lay down to sleep.

An increase in the glow of firelight entering the window told me that it was a new Argzoon 'day'. But,

I realized immediately, that was not what had awakened me.

There was someone else in the room.

Very cautiously, I stretched my cramped limbs and began to stand up, peering through a crack in my barricade.

I was astonished.

The man collecting food from the baskets was not an Argzoon. He was a man similar in build to myself, but with a pale complexion—perhaps caused by living in the sunless vaults of the Blue Giants.

His face had a strange, dead appearance. His eyes were dull, his features frozen as he mechanically transferred meat and vegetables from the baskets to a smaller basket he held in his left hand.

He was unarmed. His shoulders were bowed, his hair lank and uncared for.

There was no questioning his situation and function in the cavern-world of the Argzoon.

The man was a slave and seemed to have been one for a long time.

Being a slave he would, of course, have no love for his masters. On the other hand, how much had he been cowed by them? Could I reveal myself in the hope of receiving help from him, or would he be frightened and shout for help?

I had taken many risks to get this far. I must take a further risk now.

As silently as I could I climbed from cover and crept across the tops of the baskets towards him. He was half turned away from me and only seemed to notice me when I was almost on top of him.

When he saw me, his eyes widened and his mouth dropped, but he made no sound.

"I am a friend," I whispered.

"F-friend . . . ?" He repeated the word dully as if it meant nothing to him.

"An enemy of the Argzoon—a slayer of many of the Blue Giants."

"Aah!" He backed away in fear, dropping his basket.

I leapt to the ground and dashed towards the door, closing it. He turned to face me, his mouth trembling now, his eyes still wide in ghastly fear. It was evidently not me he feared so much as something that I represented to him.

"Y-you must go to the Queen—y-you must surrender yourself. D-do that and y-you may escape the N'aal Beast!"

"The Queen? The N'all Beast? I've heard the name—what is it?"

"O-oh, d-do not ask me!"

"Who are you? How long have you been here?" I tried a different line of questioning.

"I—I think my name was Ornak Dia . . . Y-yes, that was it, that was my name . . . I d-do not know h-how long . . . s-since w-we f-followed the Argzoon h-here and w-were led into ambush. Th-they had only sent half their strength against the lands of the south—we did n-not r-realize . . ." With these memories he seemed to remember something of the man he must have been previously, for his shoulders straightened a little and he held his mouth better.

"You were part of the force led by the Bradhi of the Karnala—is that right?" I asked him. I wondered what kind of hardships could have turned a warrior into this servile thing in such a comparatively short space of time.

"Th-that is right."

"They lured you down here where the rest of their army was waiting—it had been a calculated tactic—and when you reached the floor of the cavern-world they attacked you and wiped out your army. Isn't that what happened?" I had already guessed most of this, of course.

"Y-yes. They took prisoners. I am amongst the last of them left alive."

"How many prisoners?"

"Several hundreds."

I was horrified. Now it was plain that, as I had surmised, this move of the Argzoon had been carefully planned for years. The first force had been badly defeated, but it had severely weakened the strength of the southern nations. Secondly, the southern army's punitive force that had followed the Argzoon here had been led into a carefully laid trap and the weary warriors must have been fairly easy game for a force of fresh Argzoon warriors waiting in ambush. Then the Argzoon had put the second half of their strategy into operation, going secretly south in small numbers with the object of taking the south by surprise, beginning with Varnal. Something had disrupted this strategy—perhaps my slaying of their master-mind—and the plan had broken down. But much damage had been done. The south would take years recovering from the blow and while recovering would face constant danger from other, stronger would-be aggressors. The Vladnyar, for instance.

Now I asked the slave the leading question:

"Tell me—have two women been brought here recently? A dark one and a fair one."

"There h-has been a woman prisoner . . ."

Only one! I prayed that Shizala had not been killed on the way.

"What does she look like?"

"She is very beautiful—fair-haired—a Karnala woman, I think . . ."

I sighed with relief. "But what of Horguhl the Vladnyar—the dark-haired woman?"

"Ah!" His voice was a muted scream. "Do not mention th-that name. Do not mention it!"

"What is wrong?" I could see that he was in an even worse state now than when I had originally confronted him. Spittle ran down his chin and his eyes flickered crazily. He was trembling in every part of his body. He hugged himself, hunched and twitching. He began to moan slowly.

I seized his shoulder, trying to shake some self-control into him, but he fell to the floor and continued to moan and tremble.

I knelt beside him. "Tell me—who is Horguhl—what is her part in this?"

"Ah! P-please—leave me. I will not tell them you are here . . . Y-you must go. L-leave!"

I continued to shake him. "Tell me!"

Suddenly a new voice spoke from behind me. A cool, mocking voice full of controlled, malicious humor . . .

"Leave the poor wretch alone, Michael Kane. I can answer your question better than he. My guards mentioned a disturbance in the store-room so I came to investigate myself. I have been half-expecting you."

I whirled, still in a crouching position, and looked up to stare into the deep, evil eyes of the dark-haired woman whose rôle had been such a mystery. It was to be a mystery no longer.

"Horguhl! Who are you?"

"I am Queen of the Argzoon, Michael Kane. It was I who commanded the army you defeated, not poor Ranak Mard. My army dispersed before I could recall it because that bitch-dahara Shizala attacked me soon after you had left. In the struggle she knocked me unconscious but she was then captured by some of my men. When I awoke, my army was in confusion, so I decided to take vengeance on her instead of her city . . ."

"You! All this was your doing! But how are you Queen of those giant savages—what power can one woman wield over them?"

"It is my power over something else that they fear," she smiled.

"What is that?"

"You will learn soon enough." Blue Giants were beginning to swarm into the room behind her. "Seize him!"

I tried to stand up but stumbled against the prone and shaking body of the slave. Before I could recover my position half-a-dozen Argzoon were piling on top of me.

I fought back with fists and feet, but soon they had bound my arms behind me and Horguhl was laughing in my face, her white, sharp teeth flashing in the gloom.

"And now," she said, "you will learn the punishment meted out to the man responsible for disrupting the plans of the Queen of the Argzoon!"

CHAPTER TWELVE

THE PIT OF THE N'AAL BEAST

"**B**RING him to my chambers," Horguhl ordered the guards. "I will question him first."

I was forced to walk behind her, following her through a maze of bleak and draughty corridors lit by guttering torches, until we came to a large door apparently made of heavy wood covered with silver hammered into some crude semblance of a design.

This door was opened and the big room we entered was warmed by a huge fire roaring in a grate at one side. The room itself was rich with rugs of fur and heavy cloth. Covering the walls were tapestries, obviously booty from raided cities, for the workmanship was exquisite. Even the windows were covered, and this explained the warmth of the room.

A heavy chest, about the height of my waist, stood near the fire. On this stood jugs of wine and bowls of fruit and meat. A large, fur-strewn couch was on the other side of the room opposite the fire, and there were a few benches and carved wooden chairs dotted about.

Though not particularly lavish by the standards of the civilized south, the Queen's chambers were luxurious compared with what I had witnessed of the living standards of the Argzoon peoples.

Over the fireplace hung a tapestry much less well executed than the others. It depicted the creature I had already seen on the Queen's banner—the mysterious N'aal Beast. It looked menacing and I noticed the guards avert their eyes from it as if afraid of it.

I was still tightly bound, of course, and when Horguhl dismissed the guards she was in no danger from me. I stood straight-backed, staring over her head as she paced before me, darting me strange, curious looks. This went on for some time, but I kept my expression blank and my eyes fixedly ahead.

Suddenly she faced me, swept back her right hand and slapped me stingingly across the mouth. I kept my features rigid as before.

"Who are you, Michael Kane?"

I did not answer.

"There is something about you. Something I have never sensed in any other man. Something I could learn to—to like." Her voice became softer and she took a step closer to me. "I mean it, Michael Kane," she said. "Your fate will not be pleasant if I order it to be carried out. But you could avert it . . ."

I still remained silent.

"Michael Kane—I am a woman. A—a sensitive woman." She laughed lightly, somewhat self-mockingly, I thought. "I am what I am through no circumstances of my own making. Would you like to hear why I am Queen of the Argzoon?"

"I would like to know where Shizala is, that is all," I said at length. "Where is she?"

"No harm has come to her yet. Perhaps none will. I have thought out an interesting fate for her. It will not kill her, but it will help me turn her into a willing handmaiden, I think. I would rather keep the ruler of Varnal as my cringing slave than have her dead . . ."

My mind raced. So Shizala was not to die—yet, at any rate. I was relieved, for that would give time for Darnad to come and try to rescue her. I relaxed a little—perhaps I even smiled.

"You seem in good humor. Do you not feel anything for the woman, then?" Horguhl sounded almost eager.

"Why should I?" I lied.

"That is good," she said, almost to herself. She strode panther-like to the couch and spread her beautiful body upon it. I continued to stand where I was, but looked directly into those smouldering eyes. After a while she dropped her gaze.

Staring at the floor, she said: "I was only a child of eleven when the Argzoon attacked the caravan in which I and my parents were travelling through the northern borders of Vladnyar. They killed many—including my mother and father—but took slaves as well. I was one of those slaves . . ."

I knew she was trying to touch me in some way, and if her story were true I felt sorry for the child she had been. But I could not, considering her later crimes, justify them.

"In those days, the Argzoon were divided amongst themselves. Often the cavern was a battlefield between warring factions. They could not unite. The Argzoon were split into scores of family clans and blood-feuds were normal, day-to-day happenings. The only thing that could unite them for a short while was the common fear of the N'aal Beast which haunted the subterranean passages below the floor of the Great Cavern.

It fed on the Argzoon, who were its natural prey. It would slither up and attack then slither away again. The Argzoon believe that the N'aal Beast is an incarnation of Raharumara, their chief deity. They dared not make any attempt to kill it. Whenever possible they would sacrifice slaves to it.

"When I was sixteen years old, I was chosen as one of those who would feed the N'aal Beast. But already I had felt this power in me—some ability to make others do my will. Oh, not in large ways—I was still a slave—but in ways that made my lot a little easier. Strangely, it was the N'aal Beast which brought this power out of me in strength.

"When the news came that the N'aal was slithering up into the Great Cavern, I and a number of others—folk like myself and Argzoon criminals—were bound and placed in its supposed path. Soon it appeared and I watched in horrified dread as it began to seize my companions and swallow them. I started to stare into its eyes. Some instinct made me croon at it. I—I don't know what it was, but it responded to me. Through my mind, I was able to communicate with it, give it orders."

She paused and looked up at me. I did not react.

"I returned to this city—the Black City—with the N'aal Beast following me like a pet. I ordered a deep hole to be made, in which the beast was imprisoned. The Argzoon regarded me with superstitious awe—they still do. By controlling the N'aal Beast, I control them. Later I decided to make up for my years of misery and hardship and planned conquest of this entire continent. By several methods I got news of the south and her defences. Then I put the first stage of my plan into operation. I was prepared to wait years for victory—but instead . . ."

"Defeat," I said. "A well-deserved defeat. Your years with the Argzoon have warped you, Horguhl—warped you beyond hope of salvation!"

"Fool!" She was off the couch and pressing her voluptuous body against me, stroking my chest. "Fool! I have other plans—I am not defeated. I know many secrets; I have much power that you do not dream of. Michael Kane, you can share all this. I told you I have never known a man like you—brave, handsome, strong-willed. But you also have something else—some mysterious quality that makes you as different from the ordinary riff-raff of Vashu as I am. Become my King, Michael Kane . . ."

She was speaking softly, her hypnotic eyes staring into mine, and something seemed to be happening to my brain. I felt warm, euphoric. I began to think her proposal was attractive.

"Michael Kane—I love you!"

Somehow that statement saved me—though I will never know why. It jerked my mind back to sanity. Bound as I was, I shrugged her clinging hands away.

"I do not love you, Horguhl," I said firmly. "Neither could I feel anything but loathing for someone who has done what you have done. Now I realize how Shizala was so easily brought here—that hypnotic power of yours! Well, it will not get the better of me!"

She released me and when she spoke again her voice was low, vibrant. "Somehow I knew that. Perhaps that is what attracts me to you—the fact that you can resist my power. Few others can—not even that primordial beast, the N'aal."

I took several steps backwards. I was still looking

around for some means of escape. She seemed to realize this and looked up suddenly.

Her face was now a mask of hatred!

"Very well, Michael Kane—by refusing me you are
accepting the fate I had planned for you. Guards!"

The huge Argzoon warriors entered.

"Take him! Send messengers to all the Argzoon
who have returned. There are not many as yet—but
tell them all to come. Tell them they are going to witness a sacrifice to Raharumara!"

With that, I was led away.

I spent a short time with my guards when they
paused in a chamber near the exit of the castle. Then
they led me out through the smoky, evil-smelling
streets of the Black City. Behind us, in twos and threes
at first, then in increasing numbers, there began to follow a procession of Argzoon. One blue warrior who
strode beside my guards, keeping pace with me,
darted me a strange glance which I could not interpret. The warrior did not wear armor—I assumed he
had lost it during the flight back to the Black City—
and he had the signs of a recent wound on his breast.
Then we were passing from the city and I forgot about
him.

The scene beyond the city was like a mediaeval
painting representing Hell. The great bonfires roared,
sending flickering, smoky light across the rocky plain
that was the cavern floor. The giant Argzoon looked
like demons as they escorted me over the plain. The
fires were the fires on which the damned were roasted.
And I was soon to meet a creature very like an ancient
representation of Satan!

Horguhl was already there, standing on a dais that
was reached by a flight of about sixty steps. Her back

was turned to us and her arms were outstretched. On either side of her were braziers, flaring brightly to show her to all. The Argzoon began to form a semi-circle at the bottom of the steps, and spread out along the sides of what was plainly a pit, now that we were closer. The steps terminated at the dais and the dais looked down on the pit.

My guards halted and waited expectantly just before the first step. We all looked up at Horguhl. She was crooning something. The words—sounds, rather, for I did not recognize them—sent a shudder through me and I noticed that many of the Argzoon were similarly affected.

There came a peculiar, slithering sound from the pit and from it, just to one side of the dais, I saw a great flat serpent head rise up and begin to sway in rhythm to Horguhl's crooning.

The Argzoon muttered in superstitious fear and began to chant and sway in time to the movement of the serpent head. It was of a sickly yellowish color, with long fangs curving out of its mouth from the upper jaw. There was a stale, unwholesome smell about it, and once it opened its great jaws and gave forth a horrid hissing, revealing a gaping red maw and a huge forked tongue.

Then Horguhl's crooning became softer and softer, the swaying more gentle, the humming of the spectators almost inaudible, and then—it came almost as a shock to me—absolute silence.

Suddenly this silence was broken as from behind me there came a cry.

"No! No!"

I turned my head and saw who it was that had cried out.

"Shizala!" I shouted involuntarily. The fiends had brought her here to witness my death—that was obvious. Even from that distance I could see her cheeks were streaked with tears and she struggled in the grasp of two massive blue warriors. I tried to break away and run towards her, but my bonds and my guards stopped me.

"Stay alive!" I shouted to her. "Stay alive! Do not fear!" I could not tell her that Darnad was even now riding for civilization, bent on bringing help to rescue her. But perhaps my cry would mean something to her. "Stay alive!"

Her voice answered faintly: "Oh, Michael Kane, I—I—"

"Silence!" Horguhl had turned and was addressing her subjects as much as myself and Shizala. "Take the prisoner to the pit's edge!"

I was hustled forward and stared down to where the N'aal Beast was coiled. Its oddly intelligent eyes stared up at me—and I shuddered at this—almost with malicious humor!

"The N'aal Beast is in a playful mood today," Horguhl said from above me. "He will play with you for some time before devouring you."

I resolved to show no sign of the horror within me.

"Throw him down!" Horguhl ordered.

Bound and helpless, I was thrown into the Pit of the N'aal Beast!

I managed to land on my feet some yards away from where the huge snake-creature still lay coiled, looking at me with those terrible eyes.

And then, suddenly, from above I heard a cry and looked up. An Argzoon warrior was staring down at me—the one I had seen earlier who had looked at me so strangely. He had a sword in one hand and a battle-axe in the other. What was he doing?

I heard Horguhl shriek to her guards: "Stop him!"

And then the Argzoon was leaping into the pit to stand beside me. He raised his sword and I suddenly realized the truth of what was happening.

CHAPTER THIRTEEN

AN UNEXPECTED ALLY

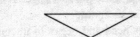

A T first I had thought that the warrior was going to slay me himself for some obscure reason. But this was not the case. Swiftly he slashed my bonds.

"I know you," I said in surprise. "You are the warrior I fought near Varnal."

"I am the warrior whose life you refused to take— whom you spared from the insults and swords of his comrades. I have thought much on what you did, Michael Kane. I admired what you did. It meant something to me. And now—I can at least help you to fight for your life against this creature."

"But I thought your folk feared it because of its supposed supernatural character."

"True. But I begin to doubt that this is true. Quickly—take this sword, I have always been a better axe-man than a swordsman."

With this unexpected—and welcome—ally, I turned to face the N'aal Beast.

The Beast seemed put out by this turn of events. Its gaze went from one to the other of us as though uncertain which one to attack first, for we had spaced out now—both crouching, waiting.

The Beast's great head suddenly whipped towards me. I stumbled backwards until I stood against the wall, desperately hacking at its snout with the great Argzoon blade.

It was evidently unused to its victims retaliating and it hissed in apparently puzzled anger as my sword gashed a wound in its snout.

It drew back its head and began to uncoil, so that soon the head had risen high above me and I was in its shadow. Down came the gaping maw and I thought it would take me in one gulp. I raised the sword point-first and as the mouth was almost upon me, the fetid breath almost overpowering, I dug the sword-point into the beast's soft palate.

It screamed and threshed backwards. Meanwhile, the Argzoon warrior had come in and hacked at the beast's head with his axe. It turned on him and the sweeping head caught him off balance.

He fell and the N'aal Beast opened its mouth, about to snap off his head.

Then I saw my chance. I leapt *on* to the N'aal Beast's back—on to its upper head and, running over that flat head, straddled it just above the eyes.

All this took only a few seconds, as the Argzoon below tried desperately to fend off the snapping jaws.

I raised my sword in both hands over the creature's right eye.

I plunged the blade downwards.

The steel sank in. The head jerked backwards and I was flung—swordless now—from my perch.

The N'aal Beast turned again towards me. The sword still protruded from its eye so that it made an even more grotesque sight as it came at me.

The Argzoon axe-man leapt up again and came to

stand by me, evidently intending to protect me now that I was unarmed.

The beast let out a chilling, reverberating scream, and the gaping mouth, forked tongue flickering rapidly, flashed down on us.

Only inches before it reached us, the head suddenly turned and flung itself upwards. The beast uncoiled its whole length and began to shoot up so that I felt it would leave the pit altogether. I caught a glimpse of spectators scattering—and then it flopped down, almost striking us and finishing us by crushing us beneath its weight.

My sword had done the trick. I had killed it. It had clung on to life longer than anything should have. I half-credited its supernatural origin then!

I bent towards the great head and removed my sword. It slid out easily.

Then I realized that nothing was really saved. I was still imprisoned and, though armed, there were some two hundred Argzoon above us, ready to destroy us at a word from Horguhl.

"What do we do?" I asked my new friend.

"I know," he said, after some thought. "There is a small opening—look there, at the base of the pit on the other side." I followed his pointing finger. He was right. There was an opening large enough to take a man but not large enough for the head of the N'aal Beast.

"What is it?" I asked.

"A tunnel that leads to the slave pens. Sometimes slaves are forced down it from the other side to feed the beast." My new friend chuckled grimly. "It will feast no more on human flesh! Come, follow me. We have slain the N'aal Beast—that will impress them.

They will be even more impressed when they see we have vanished from the pens. With luck, we shall escape in the confusion."

I followed him into the tunnel.

As we moved along it, he told me his name. Movat Jard of the Clan Movat-Tyk—one of the great Argzoon clans in the old days, before Horguhl had reorganized the Argzoon nation. He told me that though the Argzoon feared Horguhl's power, they were now muttering against her. Her ambitious schemes of large-scale conquest had come to nothing—and Argzoon was decimated.

After some time, the dark tunnel became a little lighter and ahead I saw some sort of slatted grating. It was of wood. Peering through it I saw a cavern lighted by a single torch.

Lying about on the floor, in attitudes of the utmost dejection, closely packed like cattle, naked and dirty, bearded and pale, were the remains of the great army that had been ambushed here earlier. Some hundred and fifty undernourished, spiritless slaves. I felt pity for them.

Movat Jard was hacking at the wooden grille with his axe. It soon fell and some of the slaves looked up in surprise as we entered. The smell of humanity was almost too much to bear, but I knew it was not their fault.

One fellow, who held himself straighter than the rest and was as tall as I, stepped forward. He had a heavy beard which he had endeavoured to keep clean, and his body rippled with muscle as if he had been deliberately keeping himself in training.

When he spoke his voice was deep and manly—even dignified.

"I am Carnak," he said simply. "What means this? Who are you and how came you here? How did you evade the N'aal Beast?"

I did not only address him. I addressed them all, since they were all looking at us with something akin to hope in their eyes.

"The N'aal Beast is dead!" I announced. "We slew it—this is Movat Jard, my friend."

"An Argzoon your friend? Impossible!"

"Possible—and my life is witness to that!" I smiled at Movat Jard, who made an attempt to smile back, though when he bared his teeth he still looked menacing!

"Who are you?" asked the bearded man, Carnak.

"I am a stranger here—a stranger to your planet, but I am here to help you. Would you be free?"

"Of course," he said. A murmur of excitement ran round the cavern. Men began to get up, a new liveliness in their manner.

"You must be prepared to win such freedom dearly," I told them. "From somewhere we must get weapons."

"We cannot fight the whole Argzoon nation," Carnak said in a low voice.

"I know," I said. "But the whole Argzoon nation is not here. There are perhaps two hundred warriors in all—and they are demoralized."

"Is this true? Really true?" Carnak was grinning excitedly.

"It is true," I said, "but you are outnumbered as well as unarmed. We must think carefully—but first we must escape from here."

"That should not be difficult in our present mood," replied Carnak. "There are usually more guards, but

at present there are only two." He pointed to the other
entrance to the cave. It was made of wickerwork, that
was all. "Normally the cave beyond is thick with
guards and all who have tried to escape that way have
been cut down or forced back and sacrificed to the
N'aal Beast. But now . . ."

With Movat Jard close at my heels, I strode to the
door and immediately began hacking at it with my
sword.

Movat Jard joined me, using his axe. The prisoners
crowded eagerly behind us, Carnak well to the fore.

From the other side of the door we heard a grunt
of surprise. Then an Argzoon yelled:

"Cease—or you'll be food for the N'aal!"

"The N'aal is dead," I replied. "You address the
two who slew it."

We forced the door down. It fell outwards and
crashed to the floor, revealing two baffled-looking
guards, their swords in their hands.

Movat Jard and I rushed at them instantly and had
soon despatched them in as swift a series of strokes
as I shall ever witness.

Carnak bent down and took one of the swords from
the fallen guard. Another man also took a sword and
two others helped themselves to a mace and an axe
respectively.

"We must go to the Weapon Chambers of Argzoon," Movat Jard said. "Once there, we can equip
ourselves properly."

"Where lie these dungeons?" I asked.

"Why, under the Black City. There are several entrances."

"And where lie the Weapon Chambers?"

"In the castle—Horguhl's castle. If we are quick

we can get there before they return to the city. They must be in some confusion."

"Movat Jard, why do you help us against your own folk?" Carnak asked. He seemed just a little suspicious, for he had already experienced one clever Argzoon trap.

"I have learned much from a little that Michael Kane here said, and what he did, once, for me. I have learned that *ideas* can sometimes rise above blood loyalties. And besides, it is Horguhl whom I fight, not the Argzoon. If we beat her, then I shall have to decide again what my attitude is—but not until she no longer rules the Argzoon!"

Carnak seemed convinced by this. We rushed up the slopes leading away from the dungeons and had soon reached an iron gate kept by a single watchman. When he saw us and noted, perhaps, the desperate looks in our eyes, he did not draw his weapons but flung out his hands before him.

"Take my keys—do not take my life."

"A fair bargain," I said, accepting his keys and unlocking the iron gate. "We will also borrow your weapons." Two more men were armed with a sword and an axe—making eight in all. We bound the Blue Giant and passed on into the streets.

Beyond the walls of the Black City we heard the confused babble of voices, but the Argzoon had not yet reached the gates. We headed towards the nearby castle, pouring through the streets towards the Weapon Chambers, with Movat Jard, Carnak and myself in the lead.

We swarmed into the castle, cutting down the few guards who attempted to stop us.

Just as we were breaking into the Weapon Chambers, the first of the Argzoon returned and shouted the alarm.

We burst into the Weapon Chambers, less well laid-out but not unlike the Weapon Room of Varnal in appearance, though the weapons were, of course, more barbaric.

While the joyful prisoners went to arm themselves with the best weapons of the Argzoon—not to mention the heaps of captured weapons they found lying therein—we eight, who were already armed, met the initial wave of Argzoon warriors.

We must have made a strange sight, the three of us who led—a blue man of the Argzoon nearly ten feet in height; a wild-eyed, naked man covered in hair; and a tanned swordsman who was not even of that planet. But one thing we all had in common—we could use swords.

We stood shoulder to shoulder, fending off our attackers while our comrades armed themselves. It seemed that I faced a veritable wall of swords raining down upon me from the Blue Giants.

Somehow we held them off—and succeeded in depleting our enemies.

Then, from behind us, came a great roar!

The prisoners were all armed and ready to fight. The slaves had become warriors again—warriors with a lust for vengeance for the years of servitude and fear, revenge for the treacherous ambush which had wiped out a great percentage of the flower of southern manhood.

We pressed forward now, driving the Argzoon before us!

Along the corridors of the castle we fought. In halls and rooms we fought. In Horguhl's deserted throne room we fought, and in her private rooms, too. At one stage I took the opportunity to tear down the N'aal tapestry hanging there.

Out into the streets until the whole of the Black City seethed with fighting men.

Our numbers were few. Our men had all but forgotten their old training. But our hearts were full of exultant battle-lust, for at long last we were able to strike back at our old enemies.

By the time all our force was in the streets, the Argzoon had cut down more than a third of our men—but we had taken more of them!

And the longer we fought, the more of their old skills the ex-slaves remembered. The fighting in the city became more sporadic as the Argzoon attempted to re-form.

We used the pause to check our own strength and discuss strategy. We held a large area around the castle, but the Argzoon still held most of the city.

Somewhere were Horguhl and Shizala. I prayed that Horguhl would not order Shizala slain in the pique of defeat; that the Queen still had confidence in her warriors' ability to win.

The Argzoon attacked first, but we were ready for them, with warriors deployed in every street.

For a time neither side gained any advantage. We held our position and the Argzoon held theirs.

"It is deadlock," said Movat Jard as he, Carnak and I conferred.

"How can we break it?" I asked.

"We must get a fairly large party of warriors into position behind them," Carnak said. "Then we can attack them from two sides and drive a wedge through their ranks."

"A good plan," I agreed. "But how can we move that party of warriors? We cannot fly."

"True," Movat Jard said, "but we can go *under* them. Remember the slave-pens? Remember that I said there were several entrances and exits?"

"Yes," I replied. "Could we go through one of these and emerge behind the enemy?"

"Unless they are ready for that trick," he said, "we could. But if they have blocked the entrances, we stand to lose more—since we will have a force of good warriors stranded down there unable to help defend the area we have gained. Is it worth the risk?"

"Yes," I said. "For if we do not gain an advantage soon our men will tire. They are already weak from the sojourn. We cannot afford to waste any more time."

"Who will lead them?" Carnak stepped forward, evidently thinking of himself.

"I will," I said. "You are both needed here to rally the defenders."

They understood the necessity of this.

Within a shati, I was leading a force of some thirty warriors towards the slave-pen entrance Movat Jard had indicated.

Down the winding ramps we went at a loping run.

And we ran straight into a detachment of Argzoon coming the other way!

Almost before we knew it we were wasting time and men in a battle for the underground passage.

The Argzoon seemed to be fighting with little will, and I had killed two myself and disarmed several more before the rest lay down their arms, holding out their hands in a gesture of surrender.

"Why do you give up so easily?" I asked one of them.

He answered in the coarse, guttural accent of his people.

"We are tired of fighting battles for Horguhl," he said. "And she does not lead us even—she disappeared after you killed the N'aal Beast. We only followed her because we thought Raharumara dwelt in the N'aal Beast and she was stronger than Raharumara. But now we know that Raharumara does not dwell in the N'aal Beast, else you could not have killed it. We do not wish to lose our lives for her schemes any longer—too many of our brothers have died over the years to satisfy her ambitions. Now it has all come to this—a few warriors fighting in the streets of the Black City, defending themselves against slaves! We wish a truce!"

"How many others feel as you do?" I asked.

"I do not know," he admitted. "We have not talked—too much has happened too swiftly."

"You know the fair-haired girl Horguhl brought here and who was at the ceremony of the N'aal Beast earlier?" I questioned him.

"I saw her, yes."

"Do you know where she is?"

"I think she is in the Tower of Vulse."

"Where is that?"

"Near the main gate—it is the tallest tower in the city."

We took their arms from them and continued on through the slave-pens emerging at last in a part of the city almost immediately behind the rear lines of the battling Argzoon.

We attacked at once.

With cries of surprise the Argzoon turned. Then we were locked in combat, driving through their midst in an effort to link up with our comrades on the other side.

I myself was engaged with one of the largest Argzoon I had encountered. He was almost twelve feet high and fought with a long lance and a sword.

At one stage he flung the lance at me. By chance, I grabbed it in mid-air, turned it and flung it back at him. It caught him in the belly. I finished him with my sword. If it had not been for that lucky catch, I doubt if I should have survived the encounter.

Now I could see that we were almost linked with our fellows on the other side.

Certain that the tactic had succeeded, I left my men in charge of a dark-skinned warrior who had shown skill and intelligence in the fighting, and left the fray, sheathing my sword.

I was running for the Tower of Vulse near the main gate. Here I hoped that I would at least find Shizala and make myself responsible for her safety, if I could do nothing else.

I saw the Tower soon and noted that its entrance seemed unguarded.

But I saw something else. Something that sent a shock of surprise thrilling through me.

What I saw I thought impossible—some trick of the light, some illusion.

What I saw was an aircraft tethered near the top of the tower—an aircraft similar to the one in which Shizala and I had flown when we went to the camp of the Argzoon!

How did it come to be there?

I reached the entrance of the tower and ran inside.

There I found a set of winding, stone steps leading up and up. There seemed to be no rooms in the lower part of the tower. I began to run up the steps.

Near the top of the tower I found a door. It was unbarred and I flung it open.

I felt shock as I saw the two within the room.

One of them was Shizala.

The other—? The other was Telem Fas Ogdai, Bradhinak of Mishim Tep, Shizala's betrothed.

He had one arm around Shizala and his other hand held a sword as he looked warily towards the door through which I had burst.

CHAPTER FOURTEEN

SWEET JOY AND BITTER SOR-ROW

F OR a moment I confess that my emotion was one
of dreadful disappointment rather than joy that
Shizala was safe in the arms of a protector.

I dropped my guard and smiled at Telem Fas
Ogdai.

"Greetings, Bradhinak. I am glad to see that you
have managed to keep the Bradhinaka from danger.
How did you get here? Did you hear something of
where we had gone in Narlet, perhaps? Or was
Darnad able to get word to you more swiftly than I
had supposed?"

Telem Fas Ogdai smiled and shrugged. "Does it
matter? I am here and Shizala is safe. That is the important thing."

I felt the answer rather unnecessarily oblique but
accepted it.

"Michael Kane," Shizala said, "I was sure you had
been killed by now."

"Providence is on my side, it seems," I said, trying
to hide the expression in my eyes, which must have
added—'save in the most important matter of my life'.

"I hear you've performed miracles of daring."

Telem Fas Ogdai spoke somewhat ironically. My dislike for him increased in spite of my effort to take an objective attitude to him. He was not helping me.

"Providence again," I said.

"Perhaps you will leave us for a moment," Telem Fas Ogdai said. "I would like to have some words with Shizala in private."

I would not be boorish a second time. I bowed slightly and went out of the room.

As the door closed I heard Shizala's voice suddenly scream loudly.

It was too much. In spite of my earlier encounter at the palace of Varnal, I could not control myself. I sprang back into the room.

Shizala was struggling in the grasp of a scowling Telem Fas Ogdai. He was trying to drag her towards the window to where his aircraft waited.

"Stop!" I ordered levelly.

She was sobbing. "Michael Kane—he—"

"I am sorry, Shizala, but no matter what you think of me for it, I will not stand by and see a brute handle a lady so!"

Telem Fas Ogdai laughed. He had sheathed his sword, but now he released Shizala in order to draw it.

To my surprise she ran immediately to me!

"He is a traitor!" she shouted. "Telem Fas Ogdai was in league with Horguhl—they planned to rule the continent together!"

I could hardly believe my ears. I drew my own blade.

"He threatened to kill you unless I remained silent just now," she went on. "I—I did not want that."

Telem Fas Ogdai chuckled. "Remember your bond, Shizala. You must still marry me."

"When the world learns that you are a traitor," I said, "she will not."

She shook her head. "No, a bond of the kind we made goes higher than ordinary law. He is right. He will be exiled and I with him!"

"But that is a cruel law!"

"It is tradition," she said simply. "It is a custom of our folk. If tradition is ignored society will crumble, we know that. Therefore the individual must sometimes suffer unjustly, for the sake of the Great Law."

It was hard for me to argue against this. I may be old-fashioned, but I have great respect for tradition and custom as pillars of society.

Suddenly Telem Fas Ogdai laughed again, a somewhat unhinged chuckle, and lunged towards me.

I thrust Shizala behind me and met his lunge with a swift parry.

Back and forth across the room we fought. I had never encountered such a skilled swordsman. We were evenly matched, save that I had earlier exerted myself a great deal. I began to feel that he must win and Shizala would be condemned to spending her life with a traitor she hated!

Soon I was actually retreating before a whirlwind of steel and found myself with my back not against the wall—but worse—my back was to the window. A drop of a hundred feet was behind me!

I saw Telem Fas Ogdai grin as he forced me further back. I became desperate. From somewhere I called on extra reserves of energy. In a final, desperate bid I hurled myself forward, straight into that network of flashing steel!

I took him by surprise. It saved my life and cost him his.

He stumbled backward for a moment.

I thrust rapidly at his throat. The point met flesh and he fell with a great roar of baffled rage.

I knelt beside him as the life bubbled from him. I could not save him. We both knew he was going to die. Shizala came and knelt by him, too.

"Why, Telem," she said, "why did you do such a despicable thing?"

He turned his eyes towards her, speaking with difficulty.

"It was an expedition I undertook in secret more than a year ago. I thought I would try to discover what had happened to your father. Instead, I was captured and brought to Horguhl."

"You were brave to attempt such a thing," I said softly.

"She—she seduced me somehow," he said. "She told me secrets—dark secrets. I became completely in her power. I helped her plan the final stages of the attack on Varnal. I deliberately went to Varnal at the time of the attack, knowing that I would be asked to carry a message for help to Mishim Tep and your other allies." He began to cough horribly, then rallied himself.

"I—I could not help myself. I expected you to be defeated, but you were not. Your folk learned that I had not taken the message to Mishim Tep—m-my father asked why I had not. I—I could not reply. People talked—soon it was common knowledge that I had betrayed Varnal, though—though none knew *why*. It was that woman—it is like a dream—I—I am a traitor and a fool—she—she—"

He raised himself up then, his eyes staring blankly out at nothing.

"She is evil!" he cried. "She must be found and killed. Until she is, all that we love and hold valuable on Vashu will be in danger of corruption. Her secrets are terrible—they give her an awful power! *She must die!*"

And then he fell back—dead.

"Where is Horguhl?" Shizala asked me.

"I do not know. I think she has escaped—but to where is a mystery. This cavern-world is not fully known even to the Argzoon!"

"Do you think he exaggerated—that his mind was clouded?"

"I think it possible," I said.

And then, quite suddenly, she was in my arms, sobbing and sobbing.

I held her close, whispering words of comfort into her ear. She had been through incredible hardships and terrors and had borne them all bravely. I did not blame her for crying then.

"Oh, Michael Kane—oh—my love!" she sobbed.

I could scarcely believe my ears. I felt that the day's trials had turned my brain!

"Wh-what did you say?" I asked softly, bewildered.

She controlled her sobbing and looked up at me, smiling through her tears. "I said, 'my love'," she repeated. "Michael Kane, I have loved you ever since we first met. Remember, when the mizip chased you?"

I laughed and she joined in.

"But that is when I fell in love with you," I gasped. "And—I thought you loved Telem Fas Ogdai!"

"I admired him—then," she said, "but I could not

love him—particularly after I had seen you. But what could I do? Tradition had bound me to him and I could not break with tradition—"

"Nor would I expect you to," I said. "But now—"

She put her arms around me and I drew her close. "Now," she breathed, "we are free to marry as soon as the betrothal day can be arranged!"

I bent to kiss her and then realized that I was not yet sure how the battle had gone.

"We must see how our men are dealing with the Argzoon," I said.

She knew nothing of what had happened—or at least little. Quickly I told her. She smiled again and slipped her hand in mine. "I will not be parted from you again," she said. I knew I should have left her in the tower—or better still in the aircraft, where she would be safest—but I could not bear the thought of something else separating us. The aircraft reminded me of the time we had flown together over the Argzoon camp and I asked her why she had left the security of the ship.

"Did you not realize?" she asked as we moved down the steps, hand in hand. "I wished to help you—or die with you, if that was to be. But when I got there you had already done your work and gone!"

I squeezed her hand affectionately and with gratitude. I knew the rest from Horguhl.

In the street we discovered that the Argzoon were laying down their arms, evidently losing all stomach for fighting now that they had learned their Queen had fled.

Towards us, marching in excited triumph, came a detachment of warriors headed by Movat Jard and Carnak, the ex-slave.

We waited to meet them and I felt suddenly weary as I realized that we had won and that I need do no more fighting that day.

Tired as I felt, my heart was bounding with gladness. We had won—and Shizala had promised to be mine. I wished nothing else!

Then, suddenly, Carnak came rushing forward, a smile on his lips and his hands outstretched.

"Shizala!" he cried. "Shizala—is it really you? What are you doing here?"

She looked puzzled, not recognizing the bearded man. I wondered if it was an old friend and hoped it might not be some previous fiancé or someone who would shatter my happiness!

"Carnak—you know Shizala?" I said in surprise.

"Know her!" Carnak laughed heartily. "I should think I do!"

"Carnak!" It was Shizala's turn to laugh. "Is that your name? Is it?"

"Of course!"

I watched with some jealousy, I don't mind telling you, as the older man took my Shizala in his arms. And then all was revealed in a single word.

"Father!" she cried. "Oh, father, I thought you were dead!"

"So I would have been in a very short time had it not been for this young man with the strange-sounding name—and this fierce savage, his friend." Carnak cocked a thumb at Movat Jard.

Shizala turned to me.

"You saved my father's life?" She hugged my arm. "Oh, Michael Kane—the House of Varnal owes its very existence to you!"

I smiled. "Thank you—if it did *not* exist I would be a very sad man."

Carnak patted my shoulder. "What a champion—I've known none like him in all my days—and I've known some good warriors, too."

"You are a fine warrior yourself, sir," I said.

"I'm not so bad, young man—but I was never so good as you." Then he looked regretfully at his daughter and me. "I can see that you feel—um—some emotion for one another. But you realize, Shizala, that there is nothing you can do about it?"

"What?" I was almost beside myself with horror at this. What new factor had arisen to become a barrier between my love and me?

Carnak shook his head. "There is the matter of the Bradhinak Telem Fas Ogdai. He—"

"He is dead," I said. I felt relief. Of course, Carnak knew nothing of what had happened recently. Quickly I told him.

He frowned as he listened. "I knew the lad was headstrong—and I knew Horguhl could use those eyes and that voice of hers to put anyone in her power—but I never thought that the son of my oldest friend could . . ." He cleared his throat . . . "It was, in a sense, my fault—for he came to see if I still lived, a prisoner, with the intention of saving me." Carnak—or the Bradhi of Varnal, as he was—shook his head. "We shall tell his father that he died on our behalf," he decided. "As, in an indirect sense, he did."

He looked at us and smiled. "Then you can announce your betrothal as soon as we return to Varnal, if that is what you wish."

"It is what we wish," we replied in unison, smiling at one another.

It took only a short time to round up the rest of the demoralized Argzoon and it was decided that we three—Carnak, Shizala and myself—should leave the Black City in the charge of Movat Jard, thus making the Argzoon's defeat less bitter. We announced that Movat Jard was temporary ruler of the Argzoon until some vote could be taken after a treaty had been drawn up.

Realizing that the Argzoon had been led to this situation by Horguhl's schemings, we were not as hard on them as we might have been.

Soon we were entering the aircraft, bidding farewell for the moment to Movat Jard.

Carnak took the controls of the ship and guided it through the difficult twists and turns of the tunnel leading to the open air.

Soon we were passing over the Wastes of Doom, over the stunted forests, the wide river, the wilderness and the Crimson Plain.

The journey took many days, but we spent it making plans for the future, discussing all that had passed while we had been parted.

Then soon we were hovering over Varnal.

When the city discovered who we were, it went mad with joy and we were received with great ceremony. The betrothal was fixed for the following day and I went to my old room that night in a state of tremendous happiness.

But after all this came the bitterest blow of all. It was as if Fate had decided to make me go through all those trials simply to snatch away my reward at the final moment—for, in the night, I felt a strange, familiar sensation come over me.

I felt my body seeming to break apart, felt as if,

once again, I was drawn across space and time at fantastic speed. Then it was over and I was lying down again. I smiled, thinking that it had been a dream. I felt a light on my eyes and thought it must be morning—the morning of my betrothal.

I opened my eyes and looked into the smiling face of *Doctor Logan*—my chief assistant at the laboratories!

"Logan!" I gasped. "Where am I—what has happened?"

"I don't know, professor," he said. "Your body is a mass of scars—but you've put on extra muscle from somewhere. How do you feel?"

"What has happened!" I repeated loudly.

"You mean this end? Well, it took us about seven hours, but we finally picked you up again on some funny wavelength—we thought we'd lost you altogether. Something went wrong with the transmitter. Some jamming, perhaps—I don't know."

I got up and seized him by his lab coat.

"You've got to send me back! You've got to send me back!"

"Hey—your experiences haven't done you any good, prof," one of the technicians said. "You're lucky to be alive at all. We've been working for seven hours—you were as good as dead!"

"I still am," I said, my shoulders sagging. I let go of Logan's coat and stood there looking at the equipment. It had taken me to a place of high adventure and a lovely woman—and it had brought me back to this drab world.

I was hustled away to the sick bay and they wouldn't let me out for weeks what with the doctors and psychologists trying to discover what had 'really' happened to me. I was judged unfit for work and they'd never let me get near the transmitter, of course—though I tried several times. Finally they sent me to Europe—on extended leave.

And here I am.

EPILOGUE

A ND that, substantially, was the testament of Professor Michael Kane, physicist and swordsman—scientist on Earth, warrior on Mars.

Believe it, as I believed it, if you will. Do not believe it if you can.

After hearing Kane's story I asked his permission to do two things.

He wanted to know what they were.

"Let me publish this remarkable story of yours," I said, "so that the whole world might judge your sanity and truthfulness."

He shrugged. "I suspect few will make the correct judgment."

"At least those few will be right."

"Very well—and the other request?"

"That you let me finance a *privately* built matter transmitter. Can it be done?"

"Yes. I am, after all, the inventor of the machine. It would require a great deal of money, however."

I asked how much. He told me. It would make a large hole in my income—really rather more than I could afford, but I did not tell him that. I was ready to back my faith in his story with a great deal of money.

Now the transmitter is almost finished. Kane says he thinks he can tune it to the correct frequency. We have worked like dogs for weeks to complete it, and I hope he is right.

This machine is in some ways more sophisticated than the first one, in that it is really a type of 'transceiver' being permanently tuned on this special wave.

Kane's idea is that if he can return to Mars—however many centuries in the past it lies—he will be able to build another machine there and thus travel back and forth at will. That side of it seems, perhaps, a little too ambitious, but I have developed a great respect for his scientific mind.

Will it work?

I do not yet know. As this manuscript goes to press, we still have a week or so in which to test the machine.

Perhaps, soon, I will have more to write about the Warriors of Mars?

I hope so.